British Fairies

JOHN KRUSE

Green Magic

Green Magic
53 Brooks Road
Street
Somerset BA16 0PP
England
www.greenmagicpublishing.com

Cover illustration by Mark Gotto
www.markgotto.weebly.com

Designed and typeset by K.DESIGN
www.k-design.org.uk

ISBN 9780995547858

GREEN MAGIC

Contents

✌ **Introduction** ✌

"I wonder any should laugh, or think it ridiculous to heare of Fairies, and yet verily beleeve there are spirits and witches, yet laugh at the report of Fairies, as impossible; which are onely small bodies not subject to our sense, although it be to our reason. For Nature can as well make small bodies, as great, and thin bodies as well as thicke... So there is no reason in Nature, but that there may not onely be such things as Fairies, but these be as deare to God as we. ..."[1]

The text of *British Fairies* is derived from my *britishfairies* blog on *Wordpress*, but that basic material has been expanded, rearranged and revised.

The aspects of British fairylore I choose to focus upon fall naturally into three areas – traditional beliefs on the nature of fairies and their relationships to humans; the use of fairy elements in British art and literature, especially during the romantic period, and, lastly, an examination of deeper themes in our interaction with faery: how fairy beings are a vehicle for dealing with questions of sexuality and sin.

Author Serena Roney-Dougal has argued that "poetry is the natural language of faery."[2] I endorse this sentiment and, amongst the new material added to my original blog postings, I have ensured that a large amount is drawn from Elizabethan and Jacobean literature. I give particular emphasis to these works of poetry and drama as I believe it is the last period when traditional folk belief was still widespread and widely accessed. As the seventeenth century progressed, the genuine fairy

---

1   Margaret, Duchess of Newcastle, *Poems and Fancies*, London 1653, p. 139.
2   *The Faery Faith – an integration of science with spirit*, 2003, p.51.

mythology began to decline. Authentic concepts and characters were much attenuated by the time of Blake and Keats.

Roney-Dougal also said that "The myths and legends of the fair folk are the oldest in Britain and need to be revived." She sees this mythology as "the soul" of Britain and that, through its neglect, "the spirit of Britain has gone underground."[3] I agree that our fairy lore is unique to this island and so in this book I have deliberately limited my material, as much as possible, to the British Isles. Many writers refer to Irish, Manx and Scandinavian parallels. I have consciously tried to exclude this material for the simple reason that these are separate lands, divided by bodies of water as well as language, and there cannot have been the sharing of culture and beliefs that there was within the island of Britain.

---

3   *The Faery Faith*, pp.86, 99 & 1.

PART ONE

The Character and Nature of British Fairies

The Fairy Rings

Here on the greensward, 'mid the old mole-hills,
Where ploughshares never come to hurt the things
Antiquity hath charge of – Fear instils
Her footsteps, and the ancient fairy rings
Shine black, and fresh, and round—the gipsy's fire,
Left yesternight, scarce leaves more proof behind
Of midnight sports, when they from day retire,
Than in these rings my fancy seems to find
Of fairy revels; and I stoop to see
Their little footmarks in each circling stain,
And think I hear them, in their summer glee,
Wishing for night, that they may dance again;
Till shepherds' tales, told 'neath the leaning tree
While shunning showers, seem Bible-truths to me.

John Clare

Section One

Basic Characteristics

CHAPTER ONE

Oh, that this too, too solid flesh would melt

FAIRY PHYSIOLOGY

"And I'm a Fairy, lyth and limb;
Fair ladye, view me well.
But we, that live in Fairy-land,
No sickness know, nor pain;
I quit my body when I will,
And take to it again.
I quit my body when I please,
Or unto it repair;
We can inhabit, at our ease,
In either earth or air.
Our shapes and size we can convert,
To either large or small;
An old nut-shell's the same to us,
As is the lofty hall.
We sleep in rose-buds, soft and sweet,
We revel in the stream;
We wanton lightly on the wind,
Or glide on a sunbeam."[1]

Our ancestors believed in a form of life called 'fairy'; but how exactly did they conceive these beings? What was their physical form and nature (if they had one?). How did they subsist and reproduce? Did they ever die?

---

1   From *The Young Tamlane*, Scottish traditional ballad.

Scottish Presbyterian minister, the Reverend Robert Kirk, in his classic study *The Secret Commonwealth of Elves, Fauns and Fairies*, describes them variously as "astral" with "light, changable Bodies somewhat of the Nature of a condensed cloud and best seen in Twilight"[2] and as being composed of "congealed Air," which meant that they could not be physically wounded in the "fluid, active, aethereal Vehicles" which held them .[3] Kirk was Scottish and the general Highland belief was that *sidh* were not flesh and blood but spirits who looked like men and women, albeit smaller in stature.[4] They had no solidity and a hand could pass straight through them, as if through a ghost. The same was true in Wales;[5] the popular conception was that the fairies didn't have physical bodies and so could not be caught. They lived in a materially different sort of world which would change any human who visited.[6] One Welsh account depicts them dancing on the tips of rushes, evidently being both tiny and insubstantial.[7]

Given these ideas, it is strange then that it was accepted that ordinary mortals could have physical contact with fairies – dancing with them, nursing their babies and, indeed, fathering babies upon them. Expert on fairy lore, Katharine Briggs, wrote that fairies "are apparently near enough in kind to mate with humans – closer in fact than a horse is to an ass – for many human families to claim fairy ancestry".[8] Maybe there was some distinction between the physical nature of the human sized and smaller fairies. Maybe there were regional differences or simply some inconsistency in understanding. Generally, the idea seems to be that faery folk are as real and tangible as we are: they can jostle and pinch humans, they can fire projectiles at them; in other words, faery is a parallel or neighbouring world that is just as corporeal as our own.

---

2   s.1.

3   s.7.

4   see Wentz pp.102, 104, 105, 109 & 114.

5   Wentz pp.138, 140 & 144.

6   Wentz pp.144-145.

7   Rhys p.83; this is found too in the *Fairies Fegaries*, but is clearly a traditional concept.

8   *The Fairies in Tradition and Literature* p.95.

It is also notable that fairies would steal human food (and children), so they must eat the same things as humans. Fairies can be fussy about human culinary efforts, however. We have a series of stories in which lake maidens (*gwraggedd annwn*) repeatedly rejected human suitors because the bread they offered was either overbaked or underbaked – too hard or too soft.[9] It took a fine judge of baking times to win a faery heart. We know that fairies drank wine and cider and made their own food such as bread and cakes (when making the latter they were believed, for reasons which remain unexplained, to have been very noisy).[10] There is even a record of the fairies operating their own inn near Pwllheli.[11] Nonetheless, contrary beliefs were also held: in *Cymbeline* it is said of Imogen "But that it eats our victuals, I should think/ Here were a fairy."[12]

We know that fairies have a preference for dairy products, especially their lady sovereign, who is not averse to stealing what she desires. Peasants told of "How Faery Mab the junkets eat".[13] Ben Jonson in a royal masque deploys the same theme:

"When about the cream bowls sweet,
You and all your elves do meet,
This is Mab, the Mistress faery,
That doth nightly rob the dairy
And can hurt or help the cherning,
An she please, without discerning."[14]

In Thomas Randolph's *Amyntas* of 1632, fairies rob an orchard and then declare–

"Let's goe and share our fruit with our Queen Mab,
And th'other Darymaids: whereof this theam,
We will discourse amidst our Cakes and Cream."[15]

---

9   Rhys pp.4, 28 & 30.
10   Bourne, *Antiquitates Vulgares*, 1725, c.X.
11   David Parry-Jones, *Welsh Legends*.
12   Act III, scene 6.
13   Milton, *L'Allegro*, line 102.
14   *An Entertainment at Althorpe*, 1603.
15   Act III, scene 4.

Other supernaturals shared Mab's tastes, though. Brownies and lobs would undertake their arduous labours for a simple bowl of milk or cream[16] and, according to Thomas Churchyard –

> "Rude Robin Goodfellow, the lout,
> Would skim the milk bowls all,
> And search the cream pots too,
> For which the poor milk-maid weeps."[17]

So keen, in fact, were fairies upon cream, milk and such like that they would notoriously resort to theft to obtain these items.[18]

Unfairly, it appears that fairies can eat human food without injury, whereas a human tasting their food could be entrapped for ever – see for example the Cornish tale of the *Fairy Dwelling on Selena Moor,* in which a bite of a plum or a sip of cider would be fateful.

This Cornish story of Selena Moor also points up another physiological fact: fairies appear to be poor breeders. The captive maid in the story, Grace, says that only very occasionally is a fairy child born, which then is a cause of great rejoicing. In a late nineteenth century account given by Angus McLeod of Harris, he sadly remarks that "There is not a wave of prosperity upon the fairies of the knoll, no, not a wave. There is no growth or increase, no death or withering upon the fairies. Seed unfortunate they!"[19] It is to reinforce the weak fairy gene pool that human lovers are taken.

Actual physical appearance varied from one 'species' or type of fairy to another. Some were old men, some were ugly, hairy creatures, and some were tall and beautiful women. Some were average human height, some were the size of children, some were just one foot high and some were very small indeed, minute enough to dance around a glow-worm according to one Welsh account; another describes them as being the size of guinea pigs.[20] Angus Macleod of Harris eulogised as follows:

---

16   Burton, *Anatomy of Melancholy* or Milton, *L'Allegro.*
17   *A Handful of Gladsome Verses,* 1592.
18   *Robin Goodfellow - his merry pranks* and *Ballad of Robin Goodfellow.*
19   Wentz p.116.
20   *A Pleasant Treatise of Witches,* 1634; Rhys p.215.

"Their heavy brown hair was streaming down to their waist and its lustre was of the fair golden sun of summer. Their skin was as white as the swan of the wave, and their voice was as melodious as the mavis of the wood, and they themselves were as beauteous of feature and as lithe of form as a picture, while their step was as lithe and stately and their minds as sportive as the little red hind of the hill."[21]

One Welsh female fairy, the *jili ffrwtan*, exemplified this: she was noted for both her amorous disposition and her pride.

John Rhys noted the anomalous fact that fairy maidens are generally beautiful but that changelings are usually repulsive. Sometimes the entire fairy population of an area was ugly (for example Llanfabon, Glamorgan); sometimes they are uniformly tall, fair-haired and blue eyed (for instance at Pennant, Caernarfon [22]). One notable tribute to the physical charms of fairy women is found in the early fifteenth century ballad of Thomas of Erceldoune. He meets a fairy queen under the greenwood spray:

"And, as the story tells, full right,
Seven times by her he lay.
She sayd, Man, you like your play,
What woman in a bower can deal with thee?
You delight me during this long day,
I pray thee, Thomas, let me be!"

Whatever the irresistible beauty of fairy maidens, we should be aware of the fact that fairy folk sometimes bore bodily defects that disclosed their supernatural identities. This is marked in Scandinavian folklore – for example, the *elle maidens* dancing near the elder thickets had alluring faces but were hollow behind and the *huldre folk* had cow's tails. In Britain, this is a less common theme but, for example, Highland *glaistigs* wore long dresses to cover their hooves and a few other Scottish fairies were similarly marked and their true natures betrayed.

Something should perhaps be said here as to fairy intellect. On the whole fairies are as astute as any human. Exceptions are recorded, though,

---

21   Wentz p.116.
22   Rhys c.XII; see too Cromek, Appendix F.

and these tend to focus on the household spirits, the brownies, hobs and lobs. The Scottish Brownie Clod in one story is tricked into a disadvantageous and exploitative agreement to undertake the work of two people on a farm; the Yorkshire Dobie is a notoriously dim brownie, 'willing but gullible' in the words of Katherine Briggs. Linked too with these less-bright spirits are two common story types. Fairies often conceal their names in order to preserve their power, but are as often careless of concealing them from a determined human, meaning that they are outwitted in the end. Welsh brownie *Gwarwyn-a-throt* exemplifies this: he is overheard foolishly repeating his name to himself, gloating that it is a secret – and so he is undone. A related story told of brownies and brollachans like Meg Moulach is the so-called 'no man' theme. A fairy meets a human and tells the latter that s/he is called 'ainsel' (own self). In reply the canny human replies that s/he is named 'my ainsel' or 'mise mi sen' (me myself). Some incident then occurs in which the fairy is scalded or burned. When asked by the vengeful fairy parent who was responsible the child replies 'my ainsel'/ 'mi sen' (myself) and so the clever human escapes reprisal.

Lastly, it is natural to enquire as to life span. The Reverend Kirk expressed the opinion in his *Secret Commonwealth* that "they are not subject to sore sicknesses, but dwindle and decay at a certain period, all about ane Age."[23] In other words, the fairies are not immortal. In Cornish tradition the fairies' exercise of their shape-shifting power had a serious side effect: each time they resumed their normal appearance they got smaller, so that over time they dwindled away until they reached the size of ants and were, essentially, lost. It is worth observing in this connection that in Cornwall and the South west of England, the pixie or pisky was in any case a diminutive being: the Cornish term was *an pobel vean* – the little people. Accordingly, they started at a disadvantage before they even employed their magic powers!

---

23   section 7.

CHAPTER TWO

That shrewd and knavish sprite

THE FAIRY TEMPERAMENT

Is it possible to generalise meaningfully upon the character of a people? There are, of course, popular conceptions of nations such as the British, Welsh, Irish and Cornish, but how valid are these stereotypes? Turning to supernatural realms, is it any easier to delineate temperament? Our ancestors thought so, with the denizens of faery treated as predictably uniform in their conduct and reactions rather than being individuated.

People detected distinctly discernible traits to the different 'species' of fairies. Certain identifiable types possessed very simple characters indeed, possessed of only a couple of features. For example:

- *brownies* or house elves, which were attached to specific houses or estates, were generally amenable to human proximity and were hard workers, being content with a regular bowl of gruel or fresh milk or water. Robin Goodfellow is cast in this role in Samuel Rowland's *More Knaves Yet?* of 1613; Robin helps the country wenches "To wash the dishes for some fresh-cheese hier:/ Or set their Pots and Kettles bout the fier." Brownies only became upset when presented with a more material reward, such as a suit of clothes, a mistaken kindness which would so offend that they would desert the holding or, sometimes, haunt it destructively like a poltergeist; or,

- *boggarts, bogies and bogles* and similar spirits are consistently ill-tempered, tending to mischief that shades into downright malice. By and large this is their only function – to trick, annoy and to scare, although on occasion there is a moral aspect to the treatment:

the Dorset *colepexy* was a red-eyed goblin colt that would lead wanderers astray into marshes. Sometimes this was a punishment for malefaction, such as stealing from orchards. Hobgoblins, personalised in the character of Puck in Shakespeare's *Midsummer Night's Dream*,[24] traditionally inhabit the border between brownies and bogies. They are mischievous creatures, but are generally well-disposed toward humankind and all our frailties.

The pixies and other trooping fairies, which usually take human form and often are of human stature, have more complex characters than those fairies so far described. Nevertheless, their moods, manners and motivations were fairly constant, so consistent indeed that the personality descriptions that follow might almost serve as a human's guide to dealing with Faery – what conduct to prefer, what to avoid.

The most typical fairy traits were:

- *a secretive, private disposition.* Spying and intrusion are resented and so is often chastised, frequently by pinching, as befell John Aubrey's former schoolmaster, Mr Hart, when he intruded upon a fairy dance on the downs near Chippenham. At the same time, a person who stumbles upon the fairies but stays quiet about their discovery may be rewarded for their discretion. A person who betrays fairy secrets risks "great misshapes and fearefull disasters."[25] Any risk of disclosure of their presence is hated by fairies, so that they conceal themselves with the magical power of 'glamour' and will punish severely those who breach this. A very common story across the British Isles is of the human who is midwife, nursemaid or fosterer to a fairy child. S/he is given balm with which to anoint the fairy infant's eyes, but is cautioned not to put it upon their own. The inevitable violation accidentally occurs, revealing the true nature of the fairy residence (frequently a ruin or charnel house). Later the fairies are met at the market and greeted, in response to which the eye touched with glamour is promptly blinded.

---

24 from whence the title of this chapter: Act II, scene i.
25 *The Cozenages of the Wests,* 1613.

- *piety* – poet Robert Herrick also hints at another less well-known fairy character trait: a respect for Christian superstition. In the verse *Ceremony upon Candlemas Eve* he warns maidservants to remove all the greenery that had bedecked the Christmas hall before that date otherwise "So many Goblins shall you see."

- *a strict code of morals* (for humans). As will be discussed later in chapter 18, the fairies had a clear idea how they believed that mortals should comport themselves. Observance of these principles was rewarded and disregard was firmly sanctioned.

- *kindly to those they favour*, as with the Cornish *pobel vean*, the benefits of which might include gifts of money, good fortune in their affairs and luck in love.

- *vengeful and violent* – a grudge could be harboured for generations before revenge is executed.[26] Fairies were known to be armed, just like men: the lowland Scottish belief was that they carried bows made of human ribs.[27] With these they might inflict blights with elf-shot but they might also war amongst themselves. The Reverend Kirk said that "These Subterraneans have Controversies, Doubts, Disputes, Feuds and Sidings of Parties ... they transgress and commit Acts of Injustice and Sin." As a result, they have "many disastrous Doings of their own, as ... Fighting, Gashes, Wounds and Burialls..."[28] As evidence of these conflicts, there is a Glamorganshire tradition of a fairy battle fought in the air between Aberdare and Merthyr;[29] in the Hebrides it was believed that the fairy hosts always fought at Halloween and that a red liquid produced by lichens after frost was in fact the blood of the fairy fallen.[30]

- *a love of mischief* – it was commonly known that one occupation of our 'good neighbours' was to disturb and annoy us. Fairies typically went about this in a number of ways – by:

---

26   Rhys c.VII.
27   Cromek Appendix F.
28   Kirk cc.7 & 11.
29   Sikes p.107.
30   Wentz pp.91-92.

- *making noise in houses* – a favourite activity was to disturb households during the night by making noise with the dishes and platters in the kitchen or hall.[31] Poet Thomas Heywood describes this vividly and at length. When all the pucks and hobgoblins were gathered together in a house, they would:

> "Make fearefull noise in Buttries and in Dairies;
> Robin good-fellowes some, some call them Fairies.
> In solitarie roomes these uprores keepe,
> And beat at dores to wake men from their sleepe
> Seeming to force locks, be they ne're so strong,
> And keeping Christmasse gambols all night long.
> Pots, glasses, trenchers, dishes, pannes, and kettles
> They will make dance about the shelves and settles,
> As if about the Kitchen tost and cast,
> Yet in the morning nothing found misplac't.

This sort of riot was seen as a great game, as shown by poet Michael Drayton (1563-1631) in *The Muse's Elysium:*

> "Then about the room we ramble,
> Scatter nuts and for them scramble
> Over Stooles, and Tables tumble,
> Never thinke of noyse or rumble."

Other sources of disturbance might be scraping chairs, ringing bells, laughing or playing music. Normally, though, the occupants would "come at last to be so familiar and well acquainted with them that they fear them not at all."[32]

- *leading travellers astray* – this might be done by calling out with false voices[33] or by mysterious lights. Puck especially was able to transform himself into a 'will-of-the-wisp' in order to lure people from their path. Appearing as an 'idle' or 'false' fire, Puck would wander before them, "Hovering and blazing with delusive

31   Thomas Churchyard, *A Handeful of Gladsome Verses.*
32   MS Harl. 6482.
33   *The Pranks of Puck; The Faithful Shepherdess* I, 1.

Light."[34] The victims would stray from the road, lose their bearings and end up in ponds and water-furrows, stuck in mire and clay; at which point, Puck would desert them with derisive laughter.[35] The Cornish pisky was also very prone to this mischief. The best remedy to being 'pixy-led' was to turn your coat or cloak.

- *hiding in snares* to scare farmers when they came to empty them;[36]
- *scaring people at night* by calling like owls or dogs or by appearing at windows.
- *making sleepers' clean faces dirty* by smudging them with soot;
- *tormenting livestock* – riding horses and chasing cattle. This included knotting the manes of the 'hag-ridden' steeds into 'fairy stirrups.'[37]
- *knocking on doors* and running off; and,
- *blowing out candles* at gatherings and then kissing the girls and punching the men.[38] Alternatively at parties the fairies might interrupt, perhaps by appearing in the shape of a bear or huge dog, scaring off the partygoers with the consequence that:

> "And where good cheere was great,
> Hodgepoke would come and drink carows
> And mounch up all the meete."[39]

Lastly, it will be noted that the more modern type of fairy (small, winged, associated with flowers) is a far more benign kind of nature spirit altogether. They are reserved and timid, gentle, kind, harmless and helpful. The iconography reflects this, with girlish imagery replacing wizened old men as the 'typical' fairy.

---

34   Fletcher, *The Faithful Shepherdess*, Act I, scene 1 & Act III, scene 1; Milton, *Paradise Lost*, Book ix, lines 634-9.
35   Drayton, *Nymphidia*.
36   *The Pranks of Puck*
37   Hunt.
38   *Ballad of Robin Goodfellow* and *Robin Goodfellow, his merry pranks*.
39   Thomas Churchyard, *A Handful of Gladsome Verses*, 1592.

CHAPTER THREE

All manner of odd noyses

FAIRY LANGUAGE

What language do fairies speak? If we were to ask J. R. R. Tolkien and his many admirers, we would of course be advised 'Elvish' – the languages of *Quenya* and *Sildarin* that Tolkien forged out of Finnish and Welsh. These languages are fascinating intellectual feats, but they are modern, academic inventions; they do not reflect our predecessors' views on the matter. What does folklore have to tell us about elvish speech?

The normal rule is that fairies will speak the same language as their human neighbours. Reverend Kirk states this explicitly in *The Secret Commonwealth*:[40]

> "Their Apparell and Speech is like that of the People and Countrey under which they live: … They speak but litle, and that by way of whistling, clear, not rough. The verie Divels conjured in any Countrey, do answer in the Language of the Place; yet sometimes the Subterraneans speak more distinctly than at other times."

John Rhys relayed a story of a mermaid from North Wales in which the reporter observed sceptically "we do not know what language is used by sea maidens … but this one, this time at any rate, it is said, spoke very good Welsh."[41]

This situation is to be expected, in that communication would otherwise be very difficult – if not impossible – and interaction very much reduced. Most of our fairy tales are founded upon intercourse between humans and fairies, so that mutual intelligibility is vital. The ability to

---

40   section 5.
41   *Brython,*vol.1, p.82.

converse meant that humans may overhear – or engage – in conversations [42] and also may hear or even participate in songs.[43] It follows then that the fairies speak the local language or, even dialect. They speak Gaelic in the Highlands, Welsh in Wales and English in England – and going further an Exmoor fairy sounds just like a Somerset peasant.[44]

Intelligibility is not, however, guaranteed and an interpreter may be required. In the play *Amyntas* Dorylus plays a practical joke on Jocastus, dressing up some children as fairies and telling him that "They cannot speak this language, but in ours they thank you." The pretended elves repeatedly say "Ti-ti-ta-ti" – which is, apparently, a multi-purpose phrase with several meanings. Subsequently, though, these same fairies lapse into good classical Latin. The incident is farcical, but the point to emphasise, perhaps, is that Jocastus does not necessarily find it strange that he needs an intermediary to converse with these little aliens. An interesting variant on this theme comes from the Highlands, where it was said that the bad fairies spoke English. They could be understood, therefore, though not by all and not always with ease – and they spoke a foreigner's tongue.[45]

Given a widespread knowledge that some fairies at least were of smaller stature than the human population, they have voices to match. Kirk has already implied this, but other sources are clearer on the point. At Gors Goch, Cardiganshire, little beings came to a farm house at night asking for shelter in "thin, silvery voices."[46] The pixies encountered on Selena Moor near St Buryan squeaked with little voices.[47]

Much of British fairy-lore depends upon the ability of humans and supernaturals to have contact and to form relationships. Nevertheless, the fairies' speech is sometimes said to be not only incomprehensible but may not even resemble human speech at all. One Thomas Edmund William of Hafodafel, Blaenau Gwent, met a fairy procession and "heard them talking together in a noisy, jabbering way; but no-one could distinguish the words." Other witnesses from Wales state the same: "they did not

---

42   Wentz pp.96, 101, 10, 110, 140 & 155.
43   Wentz pp.92, 98 & 112.
44   Ruth Tongue, *County Folklore*, vol. VIII, p.117.
45   Campbell, *Superstitions of the Highlands and Islands of Scotland*, c.2.
46   Wentz p.155.
47   Briggs, *Dictionary*, p.142.

understand a word that was said; not a syllable did they comprehend..." whilst in another couple of encounters we are assured "it was not Welsh and she did not think it was English."[48] In the story of Shui Rhys, who was eventually abducted by the little green fairies, it is interesting that they spoke to her "in a language too beautiful to be repeated; indeed, she couldn't understand the words, though she knew well enough what the fairies meant."[49] John Aubrey told a tale of his former schoolmaster, Mr Hart, who in 1633 came across a "faiery dance" (a green circle on the grass of the Wiltshire downs – see chapter 12) and saw there sprites who were "making all manner of odd noyses." They objected to his intrusion and swarmed at him, "making a quick humming noyse all the time." Lastly, a nineteenth century account from Ilkley of fairies surprised whilst bathing tells that they were "making a chatter and jabber thoroughly unintelligible." The noise, it was said, was "not unlike a disturbed nest of young partridges."[50] These latter descriptions bring to mind small, insect-like beings, perhaps.

Finally, we must note the very curious tale told of Elidyr by Gerald of Wales. Elidyr, as a boy, was one day escorted into an underground realm and subsequently spent much time there with the fairies. Years later, as a priest, he told his tale and, in particular, that:

> "He had made himself acquainted with the language of that nation, the words of which, in his younger days, he used to recite, which, as the bishop often had informed me, were very conformable to the Greek idiom. When they asked for water, they said *Ydor ydorum*, which meant bring water, for *ydor* in their language, as well as in the Greek, signifies water, from whence vessels for water are called *ydrie*; and *dwr* also, in the British language, signifies water. When they wanted salt they said, *Halgein ydorum*, 'bring salt': salt is called *als* in Greek, and *halen* in British, for that language, from the length of time which the Britons (then called Trojans, and afterwards Britons, from Brito, their leader) remained in Greece after the destruction of Troy, became, in many instances, similar to the Greek.

---

48   Sikes p.106; John Rhys, pp.272, 277 & 279.
49   Sikes p.68.
50   Briggs, *Tradition*, pp.133-4.

It is remarkable that so many languages should correspond in one word, *als* in Greek, *halen* in British, and *halgein* in the Irish tongue, the g being inserted; *sal* in Latin, because, as Priscian says, 'the s is placed in some words instead of an aspirate,' as *als* in Greek is called *sal* in Latin, *emi* – semi, *epta* – septem – sel in French – the A being changed into E – salt in English, by the addition of T to the Latin; *sout*, in the Teutonic language: there are therefore seven or eight languages agreeing in this one word. If a scrupulous inquirer should ask my opinion of the relation here inserted, I answer with Augustine, 'that the divine miracles are to be admired, not discussed.' Nor do I, by denial, place bounds to the divine power, nor, by assent, insolently extend what cannot be extended. But I always call to mind the saying of St. Jerome; 'You will find,' says he, 'many things incredible and improbable, which nevertheless are true; for nature cannot in any respect prevail against the lord of nature.' These things, therefore, and similar contingencies, I should place, according to the opinion of Augustine, among those particulars which are neither to be affirmed, nor too positively denied."[51]

From all that we can tell, the clerk in question appears to be concocting his elvish tongue out of elements of Welsh and Irish, with perhaps some awareness of Latin and Greek in the background. It is not, therefore, to be relied upon very much as an account of traditional beliefs. A better summary may be to say that, in general, fairies were regarded in many respects as being identical or similar to humans (not just in speech, but also in form, diet, dress and conduct). Sometimes, however, their otherworldly aspect dominated, and their speech was as alien as their magical abilities.

---

51   Gerald of Wales, *The Journey through Wales & Description of Wales*, Penguin, 1987, Book I, chapter 8 – or Sikes p.106.

CHAPTER FOUR

Of faery-lond yet if he more enquire

FAIRY DWELLINGS

Where do fairies live? This seems like an obvious question, but it is one that is not always directly asked. British folklore gives various answers to the query, in part depending on the region from whence the tale derives and in part on the nature of the fairy folk involved. It is important too in answering this question for us distinguish the places the fairies haunt or frequent, such as groves, moors, highways, stone circles and barrows, from their actual dwelling places.

A trite answer to the question of residence might be to respond that the fairies live in 'Fairyland'. In medieval times, indeed, there was a distinct conception of a parallel fairy realm, with its own society, laws, settlements and climate. The earliest version, dated to the early twelfth century, is the story of Green Children of Woolpit as told by William of Newburgh and Ralph of Coggeshall. They came from St Martin's Land where there was no sun, just a constant twilight, and the children emerged from it into the fields of Suffolk through a long cavern. Nearly a century later, and recorded by Gerald of Wales, is the tale of Elidyr and the Golden Ball. His fairyland was accessed by a dark tunnel but was an attractive place with rivers, woods and plains. The country was cloudy, yet bright, and at night very dark as there were no moon or stars.[52]

By the early fourteenth century, in the Middle English poem, *Sir Orfeo*, entry was by a rock and then:

"When he was in the roche y-go,
Wele thre mile other mo,

---

52   Gerald of Wales, Book I, 8; Sikes p.65.

He com into a fair cuntray,
As bright so sonne on somers day,
Smothe and plain and al grene,
Hill no dale nas none ysene..."

In the middle of this land stood a high castle, with walls like crystal and covered in gem stones. These lit the land like the sun.

Towards the end of the same century Geoffrey Chaucer mentioned fairyland in his own personal contribution to the tales told by the Canterbury pilgrims. The hero of this story, *Sir Thopas,* yearns to make the 'elf-queen' his sweet heart. He journeys long over dale and down, over stiles and stone walls, until "he fond, in a privee woon[53]/ The contree of Fairye/ So wilde."

Almost twenty five years later, the legend of Thomas of Erceldoune was composed. Thomas meets a fairy lady who confesses "I am of another countree." He accompanies her to fairyland, agreeing to take leave of sun and moon, of the leaves of trees and of middle earth for a year.

"Scho ledde hym in at Eldone Hill,
Undirnethe a derne [54] lee,
Whare it was dirk as mydnyght myrk,
And ever the water till his knee."

They wade for three days through this flood until they arrive at a fair orchard, full of fruit and birds, and thence to the king of faery's castle, standing amidst mountains, plains and hills.

This is the last of the great literary representations of fairyland, but the idea was by then embedded in popular imagination. In early modern Scotland the fairies' palaces under the hill were known as *Elfame* and accordingly we hear about the Court and the Queen of Elfame. For example, in a criminal trial of a suspected witch in 1576 she described the fairies thus "Thai war the gude wychtis that wynnit in the Court of Elfame" (that is – "They were the good folk that dwelled in the Court of 'Elf-home'/ fairyland.)

---

53   Meaning – *a secret place.*
54   Meaning – *secret.*

The idea lingered in folk knowledge into the nineteenth century throughout the British Isles. The Cornish story of Richard Vingoe describes how he was taken beneath Trevilley Cliffs at Land's End and found there an underground world, reached by a cavern.[55] Likewise in the Welsh tale of Einion and Olwen fairyland is accessed by an oval stone and then by a path and stairs, which are illuminated by a whitish-blue glow radiating from the steps themselves. These led to a fine, wooded, fertile country extending for miles underground and dotted with mansions and with well-watered, lush pastures. An early nineteenth century account from Nithsdale tells of a 'delicious country' with fields of ripening corn and 'looping burnies' reached by a door halfway up the sunny side of a fairy knoll.[56] Lastly, in the mid-nineteenth century in Norfolk it was still believed that in their expansive subterranean caverns the fairies built "houses, bridges and other edifices." Access to these lands might be through something as innocuous as a molehill [57] or by lifting a sod and disappearing.[58]

As will be seen in the following paragraphs, though, fairy-land in the main was seen not as a distinct and parallel realm but as supernatural 'pockets' occurring within and between the human world. The Reverend Kirk assures us that fairy dwellings are "large and fair," being illuminated by "fir Lights, continual Lamps and Fires, often seen without Fuel to sustain them." He explains one reason for our uncertainty as to the nature of these homes: they are "(unless att some odd occasions) unperceivable by vulgar eyes." In other words, they are protected by glamour and are as a rule invisible.[59]

Some writers tended to be quite vague as to exact location. For example, Reginald Scot in *The Discoverie of Witchcraft* (1584) simply stated that fairies "do principally inhabit the mountains and caverns of the earth," although their habit is "to make strange apparitions on the earth in meadows or in mountains."[60] It is possible, nonetheless, to list quite a number of typical fairy habitations:

55 See Bottrell.
56 Keightley p.354.
57 See *Round About Our Coal Fire,* 173, c.VI.
58 Wentz pp.161-163; Rhys pp.112-155 & 227; Keightley pp.298 & 306.
59 Kirk s.4.
60 Book III, c.4.

- *under or in fairy knolls* – this was knowledge held widely throughout the British Isles. For example, the distinctively rounded and richly verdant fairy *knowe* or *sithein* was prevalent in Highland tradition,[61] but it is also found in Wales: it was said that the smaller *Tylwyth teg* lived in 'holes in the hills'-[62] as did the Cornish pixies at the Gump of St Just. Welsh writer David Parry-Jones provided very circumstantial evidence as to the routes into the fairies' homes:

> "Their habitations were universally believed to be underground, in dimly lit regions, with the entrance to them under a sod, near one of their circles, by some ancient standing stone, under the bank of a river, away on the open moor hidden by bushes, or in the ruins of an old castle, as on *Ynys Geinon* rock. In the midst of this castle there was a pit with a three-ton stone lying across it, and when they wanted ingress or egress, they uttered a secret word, and lo! the stone lifted, and fell back again of its own accord. From the entrance down to the underground passage they descended along a ladder of twenty one or twenty two gold rungs."[63]

The belief prevailed in England, too; for instance, fairies lived under Hack Pen in Wiltshire, according to Aubrey. He recorded that a shepherd employed by a Mr Brown of Winterbourne Basset had seen the ground open and had been "brought to strange places underground" where music was played. As Aubrey observed of such visitors, they would "never any afterwards enjoy themselves."[64] Compare this to William of Newburgh's tale of a fairy cup, stolen from a feast in an opened barrow. It appears that any prominent or unusually shaped outcrop or hillock was likely to attract a supernatural association – for example, the Tolcarne rock near

---

61   Wentz pp.86 & 104; Campbell, *Superstitions of the Highlands and Islands of Scotland*, c.1.
62   Wentz p.148.
63   Parry-Jones, *Welsh Legends & Fairy Lore*, 1953, p.19.
64   Briggs, *Fairies in Tradition*, p.12; *Fairyist, Fairyplaces, Wessex*.

Newlyn, which was inhabited by a troll-like being.[65] The strength of the link between elves and hills may lastly be demonstrated by Rudyard Kipling's *Puck of Pook's Hill.* In the story, Puck consistently refers to his nation underground as 'The People of the Hills.' Sometimes these hills would open up to reveal a lighted hall within which the fairies danced and into which humans would be lured. This happens, for example, in Thomas Creede's play of 1600, *The Wisdome of Dr Dodypol,* in which a wine goblet is offered to a traveller by a fairy emerging from a mound in which music is being played. This enchanted realm is ruled by a wizard whose invitation is to –

> "taste the sweetnesse of these heavenly cates,[66]
> Whilst from the hollow craines of this rocke,
> Musick shall sound..."

It is the wizard's magic spell that has:

> "Made a guilt pallace breake out of the hill,
> Filled suddenly with troopes of knights and dames,
> Who daunst and revel'd while we sweetly slept..."

- *in caves and holes* – these are particularly associated with hobgoblins, for example Hob Hole and Obtrusch Roque in Yorkshire. Many Welsh tales mention the fairies residing in caves;
- *under lakes* – in Wales the *Tylwyth Teg* dwelt beneath pools and lakes, in the case of the human sized *gwragedd annwn.*[67] In light of the latter sites, we may be reassured to know that Scottish fairies sensibly preferred "Dwellings underground in dry spots" according to John Dunbar of Ivereen.[68]
- *on enchanted islands* off the Pembroke and Carmarthen coasts.[69] These disappear when approached or may only be seen by

---

[65] Wentz p.176.
[66] Meaning – *delicacies.*
[67] Wentz p.142, 144 & 147.
[68] Wentz p.95.
[69] Wentz p.147.

standing on an enchanted turf. These isles are the home of the *Plant Rhys Dwfn*. The *Tylwyth Teg* are also said to inhabit an island in a lake near Brecon which is reached by a subterranean passage leading from a door in a rock on the shore, which reveals itself once a year.[70] Another Welsh story mentions an island in a lake known as the 'Garden of the fairies;'

- *in the vicinity of standing stones* – fairies were, for example, associated with the Pentre Ifan *cromlech* in Pembrokeshire whilst in the story of *Einion and Olwen* fairyland is accessed by a path located under a *menhir*.[71] In England, it is told that the Oxfordshire fairies were last seen disappearing under the Rollright Stone circle (see chapter 26 later for more on this association);[72]

- *on the shore* – in the folklore of Newlyn and Penzance in Cornwall, the tidal shoreline is the home of one family of pixies called the *bucca*. They are propitiated by the local fishermen with offerings of fish;[73]

- *in human houses and farms* – as is very well known, brownies and similar 'house elves' co-habit with humankind (see chapter 15). For example, in his *The Hierarchie of Blessed Angels* of 1635 Thomas Heywood stated that pucks and hobgoblins were to be found living "in corners of old houses least frequented/ or beneath stacks of wood."[74] Some fairies apparently live under the human house,[75] "under the door stane," a proximity which can inevitably lead to neighbour disputes.[76] There is a story of a farmer in Gwynedd whose habit was to empty his chamber-pot outside his front door every night before bed. One evening a small man appeared and asked him to desist, as the waste was running down his chimney into his house beneath. The farmer

---

70   Parry-Jones, pp.19-20.
71   *Wentz* pp.155 & 161.
72   Evans, *Folklore Journal*, 1895.
73   Wentz pp.174-175.
74   1636, p.574.
75   Briggs pp.99-100.
76   *Border Minstrelsy* p.14.

complied, blocking up the old door and creating a new one at the opposite side of the cottage, for which he was rewarded by healthy stock and great prosperity;

- *in trees* – there are only a few traces of this association with woodland, something that seems more pronounced in Scandinavian and German tales. For example, in the *Sad Shepherd* Ben Jonson advises that –

> "There, in the stocks of trees, white Faies doe dwell,
> And span-long Elves, that dance about a poole!"

In the English fairy-tale 'The King of the cats' the nature of these tree dwellings is elaborated considerably: a wanderer at night sees a light streaming from a hollow oak; when he climbs the tree and looks inside, he discovers an interior resembling a church. From Lincolnshire comes the belief in the 'Old Lady of the Elder Tree', a spirit inhabiting and guarding these shrubs. You may also be familiar with the rhyme 'Fairy folks are in old oaks;' there is some record of a Northern belief in a race called 'The Oakmen' and pixies are said often to haunt oak trees.[77] Lastly we should note the "*ympe-tre*" of the fourteenth century ballad, Sir Orfeo. The term ymp-tree is understood to denote a grafted apple or cherry; sleeping beneath it Orfeo's wife Heurodis is approached and abducted by the Fairy King. Whether this tree is the King's home or merely a haunt of his is not clear; for certain plenty of trees were felt to have supernatural links without them being the physical residence of a fairy spirit;

- *in a ruined structure* made by glamour to look grand and well maintained. Examples are the 'Fairy dwelling on Selena moor' (actually only a derelict farmhouse) and the illusory palace on Glastonbury Tor visited by St Collen. In one fairy midwife tale, a cave is made to look finely furnished when it was really only strewn with rushes and ferns;[78]

---

77   See Hunt.
78   Rhys pp.63 & 213.

- *outside on the moors* – in Wales the *Tylwyth Teg* were said to live amongst ferns in the summer and to shelter amidst the gorse and heather during winter;[79] and, finally,
- *nowhere* – as fairies are spirit visitors to our material world, some consider that they have no habitations here. As such, they deserve human pity and comfort: a fire and clean water at night will ease their roofless wandering.[80]

Given that they have homes of their own to go to (brownies excepted) it may be surprising that fairies frequented human houses as much as they were believed to do. Nonetheless, the attraction was strong. They would come to bathe, to steal produce from the dairy or simply to cause a nuisance with noise and practical jokes (see chapter two earlier). So powerful was this imperative that it was impossible to exclude them: they would "through the keyholes swiftly glide",[81] "seeming to force locks, be they ne'er so strong."[82]

---

79   Rhys *Celtic Folklore* pp.82 & 103.
80   Wentz p.182.
81   See *Pucks Merry Pranks* and *The Fairies Fegaries*.
82   Heywood's *Hierarchie of the Blessed Angels*.

CHAPTER FIVE

Urchins, ouphs and fairies, green and white

FAIRY CLOTHING

"Wee folk, good folk, trooping all together,
Green jacket, red cap and white owl's feather."[83]

What does a fairy wear? Nowadays we may well envisage a small girl in a pink tutu with a star tipped wand. As readers may anticipate, this was decidedly not our ancestors' image of faery kind. It was, nonetheless, very much as conventional.

There were some who regarded fairies as, in many respects, indistinguishable from their human neighbours. For example, the Reverend Kirk in *The Secret Commonwealth* asserted that:

"Their Apparell ... is like that of the People and Countrey under which they live: so are they seen to wear Plaids and variegated Garments in the Highlands of Scotland, and Suanochs therefore in Ireland."[84]

Other evidence from Scotland confirms this. At her witchcraft trial in 1576 Bessie Dunlop described the fairies she had conversed with: the men dressed as gentlemen, the women in plaids; a later account of the departure of the fairies also has them attired in plaids (with red caps). An old Cornish woman described the females of the Little People as being attired like any respectable gentlewoman, in hooped petticoats, furbelows, trains, fans and feathers.[85] The 'Old woman of the mountains'

---

83   William Allingham, *The Fairies*, 1850.
84   chapter five.
85   See Hunt.

from Monmouthshire lured people out of their way in the guise an old peasant dressed in simple grey clothes and carrying milk. Other Monmouthshire fairies met in procession by one witness were led by a woman in traditional Welsh costume of high-crowned hat and red jacket, whilst the men in her train were notable for their white cravats.[86]

More commonly, there was always something about their dress which betrayed fairy-kind to the humans who encountered them. Sometimes it was the style of the garments, for example in the Highlands clothes and hats were said to be unusually ruffled;[87] more often it was the colour that betrayed them. In Cornwall, the typical appearance of the *pobel vean* was "dressed in bright green nether garments, sky-blue jackets, three cornered hats on the men and pointed ones on the ladies, all decked out with lace and silver bells."[88] There is, then, a resemblance to (antique) human fashions combined with distinctive hues. This tendency to dress in the style of a century before is underlined by the story of the fairy market on Blackdown near Taunton – "Their habits used to be of red, blue or green, according to the way of old country garb, with high crowned hats."[89]

The quintessential and identifying fairy hue was green. For example, John Campbell of Barra in the Highlands told a story of a woman seen dressed in green, observing "no woman would be clad in such a colour except a fairy woman." Indeed, the 'green gowns' was a fairly common euphemism employed to avoid too closely naming the good neighbours (see chapter 19). In about two thirds of the cases where the colour of garments is noted in an account, it is green. An account from 1725 states that they were "always clad in green" and, whilst this overstates the popular view, accounts from Cornwall through Wales and northern England and up to the Highlands repeatedly confirm the fairy preference.[90] In his *Remains of Nithsdale and Galloway Song* Robert Cromek embellished this slightly, describing "mantles of green cloth inlaid with flowers" and "green pantaloons buttoned with bobs of silk and sandals of silver." There

---

86   Sikes pp.49 & 110.
87   Campbell, *Superstitions of the Highlands and Islands of Scotland*, c.1.
88   William Bottrell, *Traditions and Hearthside Stories of West Cornwall*, 3rd series.
89   Keightley p.294.
90   Bourne, *Antiquitates Vulgares*, c.X.

are accounts of Highland fairies in kilts, but these were green and were matched by green conical hats.[91]

Some readers may recall that green was the skin tone of the mysterious 'fairy' children discovered at Woolpit in Suffolk in the 1100s. Professor Katherine Briggs has suggested that the colour relates to death – and there may be something in this. Identity with nature and plant life might be another association.

Popular as green was, it was by no means exclusive. Other traditional choices were:

- *red* – Welsh fairies were reported to dress in "gaudy colours (mostly red)" or in "soldiers' clothes" with red caps. Pixies at Land's End wore red cloaks.[92] Welsh witnesses in Victorian times often referred to the *Tylwyth Teg* as 'the red coats' by way of euphemism.[93] We also hear of scarlet and pink garments;[94]
- *white* – in Wales the *Tylwyth Teg* were 'always' clothed in white and Thomas Heywood in his *Hierarchie of the blessed angels* employs 'white nymphs' as a euphemism for the fairies.[95] Ben Jonson in *The Sad Shepherd* makes reference to "white fays" living in trees and it was said that thousands of 'white fairies' danced upon Craig-y-Ddinas in the Brecon Beacons.[96] Today, our conventional ghost is draped in a white sheet, suggesting again some link to death and the land of the dead;
- *blue* – for example, the Tylwyth Teg seen at the 'Place of strife,' Trefeglwys, Llanidloes, Montgomeryshire, were described as "the old elves of the blue petticoats;" goblins of the same parish wore blue trousers and fairies encountered dancing near Pontypool, Monmouthshire, wore blue and green aprons.[97] In the Suffolk

91 Campbell, *Popular Tales of the West Highlands*.
92 Wentz pp.142, 155 & 181; Hunt in *Popular Romances* reports an old woman at Penberth Cove who was visited by the *pobel vean*, whom she described as being like "little sodgers" in green with red and blue caps with feathers.
93 Rhys pp.44 & 137.
94 Sikes pp.12, 80 & 83).
95 Wentz p.143; Heywood p.507.
96 Sikes p.94.
97 Sikes chapter V, part iv & pp.61 & 82.

story, *Brother Mike*, the fairies appear in blue coats, yellow breeches and red caps;

- *yellow* – generally this colour only appears in the more fanciful and elaborated accounts, such as *Brother Mike* in the previous paragraph (and see Angus Macleod later). Nonetheless, Milton in his *Ode on the Morning of Christ's Nativity* speaks of "the yellow skirted fays, [that] Fly after the night-steeds, leaving the moon-loved maze." If this is more than mere poetic licence, we may have another trace of traditional belief here;

- *other* – on Shetland the 'grey neighbours' are grey clad goblins. Welsh *coblynau* haunting mines and quarries appropriately dressed in black, whereas in contrast fairies seen dancing in a barn at Llanhiddel, near Blaenau Gwent, were dressed in "striped clothes, some in gayer colours than others."[98] Walter Scott recorded Border fairies clad in "heath brown or lichen dyed garments." The fairy women of Cardigan dressed "gorgeously in white, while the men were content with garments of a dark grey colour, usually including knee-breeches." Meanwhile, around the River Teifi, the fairy women were said to dress "like foreigners, in short cotton dresses reaching only to the knee-joint." This was exceptional, as generally fairy dresses had very long trains and local girls who dressed in a more showy fashion would be likened to the *Tylwyth Teg*.[99] At the other extreme, some supernatural beings traditionally abandon human clothing altogether and appear dressed in skins or leaves.[100] In the hands of poets, an opposite tendency applies and clothing can become highly elaborate and literary. For instance John Beaumont in 1705 decked out his fairies in "loose Network Gowns, tied with a black sash about their middles, and within the Network appeared a Gown of a Golden Colour... they had white Linnen Caps on, with lace about three Fingers breadth, and over it they had a Black loose Network Hood."[101]

---

98   Sikes pp.133 & 113.
99   Rhys pp.246, 246 & 251.
100   Briggs, *Dictionary*, pp.110-11.
101   *A Treatise of Spirits*.

To summarise the matter of preferred clothing colours, we may quote the words of John Walsh of Netherbury, Dorset. In 1566 he was suspected of witchcraft and gave evidence, telling his inquisitors "that there be iii kinds of fairies – white, green and black. Whereof the blacke fairies is the worst…"

Lastly, some supernaturals, the hobgoblins and brownies, did without clothing entirely, relying on their hairiness or coarse skin. For them, the gift of clothes was the ultimate insult which drove them away from their chosen home. You may recall Dobby the house elf of Hogwarts School, dressed in an old tea-towel. Joanne Rowling knew her folklore (see chapter 15).

Authors and artists aside, the folklore conception of fairy dress was of relatively simple garments. Susan Swapper of Rye told her 1610 witchcraft trial that the fairy woman she met dressed in a 'green petticoat' and plainness seems to be the norm – as in the common accounts of 'long green robes.' Sometimes something more elaborate is suggested; Angus Macleod of Harris in 1877 relayed his mother's description of fairies dancing: "Bell-helmets of blue silk covered their heads, and garments of green satin covered their bodies and sandals of yellow membrane covered their feet."[102]

A particular identifying feature, indeed, was the fairy's cap. It is regularly mentioned, most often red, although blue and yellow are also recorded, and again allusions occur from the south-west through Wales and the north-west up into Scotland. Sometimes, as with other clothes, local fashions are worn: Highland fairies wore blue bonnets.[103] More often the style of headgear is distinctive. The shape is often pointed or conical – for example, a mid-twentieth century encounter near Perth was with a "wee green man with peakit boots and a cap like an old gramophone horn on his head." The same informant ten years later had a rather more prosaic sighting of two small men in bowler hats… The fairies of Frennifawr Mountain in Pembrokeshire had notable headgear: the men a red tripled cap and the women a "light fantastic headdress which waved in

102   Wentz p.116.
103   J G Campbell, *Popular Tales of the West Highlands*, vol.2.

the wind."[104] More simply, a Scottish account tells of a fairy troop riding, most of the riders having their hair done up in green scarves, although their leader's long hair was bound with a band glinting like the stars.[105] Other elves, spied dancing in Denbighshire, had also tied up their hair with red handkerchiefs.[106]

By the twentieth century, conceptions of the style of fairy clothing had shifted away from the traditional forms to something much more influenced by art – both high and popular. Strains of whimsy and of floaty, flimsy ballerina type garments became pervasive, as typified perhaps by Cicely Mary Barker, whose fairies were, in the main, genteel young ladies, dressed perhaps for an Edwardian fancy dress party.

To summarise, descriptions of fairy clothing tended to fall into one of three categories:

- the otherness of the fairies was emphasised by the brightly coloured and elaborate nature of their attire;
- likewise, their otherness was indicated by the fact that they wore clothes of an earlier era: to the Victorians they appeared dressed in the fashions of mid-eighteenth century Georgians, and so on; or,
- by way of contrast, the very vicinity and intimate proximity of the 'good neighbours' was shown by the fact that they wore garments almost identical to those of human kind.

Lastly, readers will doubtless have observed how long-established one image is: the pixie or gnome dressed in his green jacket and red, pointy cap is deeply ingrained in the British imagination.

---

104   Sikes p.83.
105   Keightley p.355.
106   Sikes p.28.

CHAPTER SIX

I will diminish and go into the west

THE FATE OF THE FAIRIES

Fairy-kind has always had a strong association with the past. In the previous chapter on clothing, I noted the common tendency to see fairies in antiquated fashions typical of earlier eras. This temporal distance seems to have had the function of emphasising or marking their separation from humankind.

Fairies are 'things of the past' in another sense: they have frequently been thought of as a race that is no more seen or that has departed from these lands. By way of illustration of this, Katherine Briggs entitled one of her books 'The Vanishing People.' Some readers may also call to mind the fact that Tolkien concludes *Lord of the Rings* with a departure of the elves into the west. He built upon well-established foundations.

This idea that fairies have disappeared or are no longer present in Britain has been a feature of our fairy-lore for many centuries. Chaucer, for example, had the Wife of Bath on her journey to Canterbury begin her story thus:

"In th'olde dayes of the king Arthour,
Of which that Britons speken greet honour,
All was this land fulfild of fayerye.
The elf-queen, with hir joly companye,
Daunced ful ofte in many a grene mede;
This was the olde opinion, as I rede,
I speke of manye hundred yeres ago;
But now can no man see none elves mo."

By the late sixteenth century most authors appeared to be of the opinion that fairy knowledge was no longer current amongst the educated classes. A Cornish rhyme regrets how fairies and witches had disappeared since "The world has grown so learn'd and grand."[107] An illustration of the result of the decay of traditional knowledge is found in Fletcher's play *The Faithful Shepherdess* in which a character expresses the view that:

"Methinks there are no goblins, and men's talk
That in these Woods the Nimble Fairies walk
Are fables."[108]

Samuel Rowlands in *More Knaves Yet?* wrote of 'Ghoasts and goblins':

"In old wives daies, that in old time did live
(To whose odde tales much credit men did give)
Great store of goblins, fairies, bugs, night-mares,
Urchins, and elves, to many a house repaires.
Yea far more sprites did haunt in divers places,
Then there be women now weare devils faces.
Amongst the rest was a Good Fellow devill,
So called in kindnes, cause he did no evill,
Knowne by the name of Robin (as we heare), ...
But as that time is past, that He-bin's gone,
He and his night-mates are to us unknown..."

The disbelievers were not just scholars and courtiers, though: any urban dweller who could read might consider themselves above such superstitions. Popular pamphlets demonstrate this attitude: *Robin Goodfellow, his mad pranks* for instance distances itself from any serious belief in its subject matter by speaking of "times of old, when fayries used/ to wander in the night." This was a simpler, more credulous era, when 'people ate more, drank less and were more honest.' Thomas Churchyard recalled–

---

107   Bottrell, 3rd series.
108   Act III, scene 1.

> "How old, thin-faste wives
> That rosted crabs by night
> Did tell of monsters in their lives
> That now prove shadows light."

He lists all the supernaturals beings that they had feared – 'hobgoblings, bogges, pogges and spreetes' – but fondly shakes his head:

> "These are but fabuls faind,
> because true stories old,
> In doubtful days are most disdained,
> Then any tale is told."[109]

Nevertheless, Drayton acknowledges that there will be some, like Churchyard's elderly widows, who persist in these illogical beliefs. Some are:

> "talking of fairies still,
> Nor never can have their fill,
> As they are wedded to them.
> No tales of them
> Their thirst can slake,
> So much delight in them they take."[110]

This was the paradox for those producing works like *Robin Goodfellow, his mad pranks*: on the one hand they deprecated fairy belief as outmoded and gullible, yet they knew there was a paying market for such material.

As I suggest, the citations given so far probably reflect the urban, educated, cultured view, in contrast to the beliefs of 'simple' country folk, but traditional folk tales have also featured and explained the reduction in the sightings of our supernatural neighbours. For example, there is the Scottish story of '*The Departure of the Fairies*' recounted by Hugh Miller.[111]

> "On a Sabbath morning, all the inmates of a little hamlet had gone to church, except a herd-boy, and a little girl, his sister, who were lounging

---

109 *A Handeful of Gladsome Verses*, 1592.
110 Drayton, *Nymphidia*.
111 *The Old Red Sandstone*, p. 251.

beside one of the cottages, when just as the shadow of the garden-dial had fallen on the line of noon, they saw a long cavalcade ascending out of the ravine, through the wooded hollow. It winded among the knolls and bushes, and turning round the northern gable of the cottage, beside which the sole spectators of the scene were stationed, began to ascend the eminence towards the south. The horses were shaggy diminutive things, speckled dun and grey; the riders stunted, misgrown, ugly creatures, attired in antique jerkins of plaid, long grey clokes, and little red caps, from under which their wild uncombed locks shot out over their cheeks and foreheads. The boy and his sister stood gazing in utter dismay and astonishment, as rider after rider, each more uncouth and dwarfish than the other which had preceded it, passed the cottage and disappeared among the brushwood, which at that period covered the hill, until at length the entire rout, except the last rider, who lingered a few yards behind the others, had gone by. "What are you, little manie? and where are ye going?" inquired the boy, his curiosity getting the better of his fears and his prudence. "Not of the race of Adam," said the creature, turning for a moment in its saddle, "the people of peace shall never more be seen in Scotland."‘

Seemingly, the fairies were in headlong retreat across Britain, including in the more amenable 'Celtic fringe.' Describing Cornwall in the first decades of the nineteenth century, one historian had to admit that:

> "The age of piskays, like that of chivalry, is gone. There is perhaps at present hardly a house they are reputed to visit ... The fields and lanes are forsaken. Their music is rarely heard."[112]

Touring Wales in late Victorian times, Professor John Rhys was several times told that fairies were no longer encountered in the countryside. They had been seen 'daily' by shepherds "in the age of faith gone by," in the "fairy days" – but no more.[113] The reasons given for the fairies' departure tend to be related but curiously antagonistic:

---

112   Hitchins F., *A History of Cornwall from the Earliest Records*, 1824.
113   Rhys, pp.115 & 125.

- they are driven away by the sound of new church bells;[114]
- they had fled the spread of agriculture. Given the fairy aversion to iron (see chapter 24), it was said in South West Scotland that wherever the plough had cut the turf or the scythe had severed the crops, the fairies would not return again.[115]
- they have been displaced by the clergy (in Chaucer's plainly satirical lines):

> "For now the grete charitee and prayeres
> Of limitours and othere holy freres, …
> This maketh that ther been no fayeryes.
> For ther as wont to walken was an elf,
> Ther walketh now the limitour him-self;"[116]

- they have been deliberately exorcised: it was explained to John Rhys that the fairies did not appear as in a "former age" because they had been cast out (*ffrymu*) for a period of centuries and would not be back during 'our time.'[117] It is interesting that this ejection, albeit long, was considered a temporary state – a reason for some to be hopeful, perhaps; or,
- they have left because the catholic faith had been replaced. Herrick alleged that "if their legend doe not lye/ They much affect the Papacie" and that "Theirs is a mixt religion/ And some have heard the elves call it/ Part pagan, part papisticall."[118] As a result of these sympathies, the Reformation drove them out:

> "Was then a merrie world with us
> When Mary wore the crowne,
> And holy water sprinkle,
> was believed to put us down."[119]

---

114 see for example Briggs, *Dictionary*, p.95.
115 Cromek Appendix F.
116 Wife of Bath's tale.
117 pp.221/228.
118 *The Fairie Temple.*
119 *The Shepherd's Dream*, 1612.

The rise of Protestantism was seen, in part, to have ushered in an era of reason after "the benighted age of Popery." The Reformation therefore marked a time when belief that:

> "*Hobgoblins* and *Sprights* were in every *City* and *Town* and *Village*, by every *Water* and in every *Wood*, was very common. But when that Cloud was dispell'd, and the Day sprung up, those Spirits which wander'd in the Night of Ignorance and Error, did really vanish at the Dawn of Truth and the Light of Knowledge."[120]

Much more recently, in his story *The Dymchurch Flit*, Rudyard Kipling ascribes the fairies' flight to the ill-will generated by religious dissension and the sense that they were no longer welcome and did not belong: "Fair or foul, we must flit out o' this, for Merry England's done with, an' we're reckoned among the Images."[121] The poem, *Farewell, Rewards and Fairies*, by Richard Corbet (1582–1635) is mentioned in the same book by Kipling and encapsulates these ideas. Here is one stanza, but see the whole poem in Appendix Two:

> "... the Fairies
> Were of the old Profession.
> Their songs were 'Ave Mary's',
> Their dances were Procession.
> But now, alas, they all are dead;
> Or gone beyond the seas."

The combined shrinking and retreat of fairies and their realms reached a point in the twentieth century where many writers could declare their epitaphs. For example, in *Puck of Pook's Hill*, published in 1908, Rudyard Kipling has his character Puck admit that:

---

120 Bourne, *Antiquitates Vulgares*, 1725, c.X, p.84.
121 *Puck of Pook's Hill*, p.267.

"The People of the Hills have all left. I saw them come into Old England and I saw them go. Giants, trolls, kelpies, brownies, goblins, imps; ... good people, little people ... pixies, nixies and gnomes and the rest – gone, all gone!" [122]

Another writer in 1900 felt it was necessary only to say simply that brownies "are now extinct, as well as the Fairies."[123]

Katherine Briggs began the first chapter of *The Fairies in Tradition and Literature* by observing how, since the late Middle Ages at least, fairy beliefs "have been supposed to belong to the last generation and to be lost to the present one," but noting too how still the tradition lingered on. However, she seemed to have lost heart in *The Anatomy of Puck*, admitting that "the fairies, who descended perhaps from gods older than those the druids worshipped, who were so long lamented as lost and so slow to go, have gone, now and forever."[124]

Nevertheless, the announcement of the demise of faery may have proved premature. As Janet Bord wrote that "the changes that have occurred in this century have not resulted in the complete extinction of the fairies: they have survived, because people still see them."[125] The changes to which she referred are the impact of technology, the loss of importance of traditional beliefs and the loss of traditional knowledge. The cultural influences of the media – and a decline in sympathy with the natural environment – have led to a diminution in fairy belief, but not its destruction. For many people, "fairy lore is still alive in the background of their existence."

The rise of alternative spiritualities has definitely contributed to this tenacity of belief. In his book on the Cottingley fairy photographs, *The Coming of The Fairies,* Sir Arthur Conan Doyle quoted with approval from the writings of Theosophist Edward Gardner. The latter stated that:

---

122 p.10.
123 Brand, *Popular Antiquities*, p.116.
124 p.11.
125 *Fairies – Real Encounters with Little People* (1998).

"For the most part, amid the busy commercialism of modern times, the fact of their existence has faded to a shadow, and a most delightful and charming field of nature study has too long been veiled. In this twentieth century there is promise of the world stepping out of some of its darker shadows. Maybe it is an indication that we are reaching the silver lining of the clouds when we find ourselves suddenly presented with actual photographs of these enchanting little creatures – relegated long since to the realm of the imaginary and fanciful."

Gardner, Doyle and Geoffrey Hodson all waxed lyrical in the early decades of the century about beings existing at 'higher levels of vibrations' and similar. They renewed the foundations for a belief in the existence and visibility of fairies which persists. Diane Purkiss, in her book *Troublesome Things,* was harsh on modern manifestations of fairy belief. She wrote scathingly that a "few sad, mummified Victorian fairies survive, pressed in the pages of the *Past Times* catalogue, perhaps. Some people are devoted to these little corpses, tending them devotedly, but they obstinately refuse to flourish, they have no roots and no branches, no real resonance." She rejected these remnants as being mere "revenants, wraiths, sad simplified ghosts." [126]

I will leave it to readers to decide on the validity of these dismissive words. A glance at the abundance of fairy websites, and the shops and magazines offering a wealth of fairy related products, must give some reason to doubt Purkiss' scorn. It would not be wrong to agree with Katherine Briggs that fairy tradition at least lingers, even today; perhaps, in fact, a more vigorous verb is justified – burgeons, perhaps?

---

126   chapter 10.

CHAPTER SEVEN

Even lovers drown

MERMAIDS AND FAERY

"A mermaid found a swimming lad,
Picked him for her own,
Pressed his body to her body,
Laughed; and plunging down
Forgot in cruel happiness
That even lovers drown."[127]

It is not, of course, possible to undertake a serious taxonomy of imaginary beasts, but personally I have never considered mermaids to be fairies: they cannot disappear, they have no magical powers (mostly) and they are often at the mercy of humans. They seem too solid and physical. They are semi-human, with some supernatural qualities, but they are not in the same dimension as fairies, I would contend, even allowing for the fact that fairies are terrestrial whilst mermaids are marine.

As stated, a phylogeny of creatures that are the products of mythology rather than biology is futile, but we can still offer some sort of classification and analysis:

- *mermaids and mermen* are part human, part fish and are found around the coasts of England and Wales;
- *seal people* including the *selkies* of Orkney and Shetland and the *roane* of the Highlands and islands are humans who can assume a seal skin to move through the sea. Comparable are the *merrows* of Ireland.

---

127   W. B. Yeats, 'The Mermaid' from *The Tower*, 1928.

Mermaids and seal people are often captured and made into the wives of human males, the mermaids by being stranded at low tide and the seal maidens by having their seal skins found and hidden after they have shed them on the shore. These wives always pine for the sea and, eventually, always escape back to it. Ashore, mermaids are usually helpless and are at the mercy of the men who find them. If they are assisted back into the sea, they may well grant magical protection to their saviours; if aid is refused, the men may be cursed. The lure of mermaids for men appears to be their semi-naked state, their beauty – and most notably their hair – and their strange gnomic sayings, which added to their mysterious aura. A mermaid encountered on a rock near Porth y Rhiw in South Wales said simply "Reaping in Pembrokeshire and weeding in Carmarthenshire" before heading beneath the waves. Another caught near Fishguard advised "Skim the surface of the pottage before adding sweet milk. It will be whiter and sweeter and less of it will do." It is not explained why an aquatic being should offer culinary advice.[128]

Doubtless mermaids and fairies both were blamed by our ancestors for sudden and inexplicable illness (see too chapter 20) and storms, drownings and disappearances. There must, too, be some measure of anthropomorphising of seals, glimpsed floating in the waves and mistaken for humans.

Generally, mermaids lack magical abilities, although their deaths may provoke (or be avenged by) storms. In some cases they can control the waves by their words; in other instances their power is not innate but derives from an article such as a cap or a leather mantle.

Some mermaids, beautiful as they may seem, are in truth monsters that lure fishermen to their deaths. For Yeats, as seen in the verse above, this may be through a combination of accident and neglect. Sometimes, too, these unions need not be tragic, as with the mermaid of Zennor in Penwith who lured away Mathey Trewella to live with her; he was lost to his human friends and relations but apparently did not perish, living happily ever after beneath the waves. Indeed, Cornish mermaids are generally more fairy-like in their attributes. In the story of 'Lutey and the mermaid' a fisherman of Cury on the Lizard was granted three

---

128   Rhys p.166.

wishes by a stranded mermaid whom he rescued. Likewise in the 'Old man of Cury' a mermaid found and returned to the waves at Kynance Cove provided a magical comb by which she could be summoned to provide arcane knowledge to her saviour.

Mermaids and *selkies* are strictly salt water beings. A variety of fresh water spirits or monsters are identified by folklore, such as Jenny Greenteeth who drags children into ponds, and kelpies; there are also marine monsters. All of these have only one characteristic – destroying human life – and they lack any personality and society like fairies 'proper.' There are two diametrically opposed exceptions:

- in north-west England is found the *Asrai*, an aquatic fairy occasionally dredged naked and helpless in nets from pools and lakes, but which melts away in the air very quickly; and,
- in Wales the *Gwragedd Annwn* are lake maidens who emerge from inland waters and occasionally marry young men – but always on their own terms and subject to their own conditions, which are ultimately always breached by their husbands, causing the water fairy to return home forever.

Wirt Sikes in *British Goblins* devoted his third chapter to the *gwragedd annwn*, recounting various folk tales and, in passing, observing that these fresh water sprites exist in the absence of mermaids in Welsh mythology. Katherine Briggs provides full details of all these stories and others concerning selkies in her *Dictionary of Fairies*; she also directs readers to *Sea Enchantresses* by Gwen Benwell and Arthur Waugh.[129]

---

129   London 1961.

Section Two

Fairy Attributes

CHAPTER EIGHT

Queen Mab hath been with you

THE FAIRY QUEEN

Mab, 'Queen' of the fairies, is a very well-known name in literary fairy land, thanks amongst others to Shelley (who calls her 'Queen of Spells'), Drayton, Shakespeare, and Randolph, who in his play *Amyntas* makes her wife of Oberon and a "beauteous empress" reigning in faery. In this chapter I want to outline her traditional character.

Mab was generally conceived as being a tiny creature – the archetypal fairy. She is believed to be derived from the Welsh Mabb, queen of the *ellyllon*, who were minute elves of grove and vale. The most famous account of her is in *Romeo and Juliet*, when Mercutio describes her in the following terms:

"She is the fairies' midwife, and she comes
In shape no bigger than an agate stone
On the forefinger of an alderman,
Drawn with a team of little atomi
Over men's noses as they lie asleep.
Her wagon spokes made of long spinners' legs,
The cover of the wings of grasshoppers,
Her traces of the smallest spider's web,
Her collars of the moonshine's watery beams,
Her whip of cricket's bone, the lash of film,
Her wagoner a small gray-coated gnat,
Not half so big as a round little worm
Pricked from the lazy finger of a maid.
Her chariot is an empty hazelnut

Made by the joiner squirrel or old grub,
Time out o' mind the fairies' coachmakers.
And in this state she gallops night by night
Through lovers' brains, and then they dream of love;
On courtiers' knees, that dream on curtsies straight;
O'er lawyers' fingers, who straight dream on fees;
O'er ladies' lips, who straight on kisses dream,
Which oft the angry Mab with blisters plagues,
Because their breaths with sweetmeats tainted are.
Sometime she gallops o'er a courtier's nose,
And then dreams he of smelling out a suit.
And sometime comes she with a tithe-pig's tail
Tickling a parson's nose as he lies asleep,
Then he dreams of another benefice.
Sometime she driveth o'er a soldier's neck,
And then dreams he of cutting foreign throats,
Of breaches, ambuscadoes, Spanish blades,
Of healths five fathom deep, and then anon
Drums in his ear, at which he starts and wakes,
And being thus frighted swears a prayer or two
And sleeps again. This is that very Mab
That plaits the manes of horses in the night
And bakes the elflocks in foul sluttish hairs,
Which once untangled, much misfortune bodes."[130]

This diminutive stature is compounded by Shelley in his poem *Queen Mab* by an insubstantial and wispy physical form.

Whatever her size, though, Mab is a source of disturbance for humans. She is mischievous, interfering in the stables, undoing domestic chores and pinching and tormenting lazy servants – for example Ben Jonson in his 1603 'Entertainment at Althorpe' warns that in the dairy Mab can hinder the churning. As seen earlier in chapter 1, she seems particularly fond of dairy products and is particularly prone to stealing them. She is made, too, one of the main ministers of fairy justice (see chapter 18).

---

130   Act One, scene 4.

Secondly, she becomes the archetype of the sensual, sexual fairy. Mercutio describes her as the fairy midwife of dreams and she enables sleeping humans to realise their desires in fantasy. The fairy queen herself is passionate and is closely linked with sex and love. Robert Herrick, in his poem *Oberon's Palace,* tells of a naked and "moon-tanned" Mab who goes to bed with the elf-king. It was widely believed that she would fall for young men and choose them as her lovers.[131]

This interference in human affairs is taken one stage further, though, according to Mercutio's description, and in this final aspect we find a link to the sensual, sexual fairy that I will discuss later in chapters 31 and 34. Romeo's companion also recounts that

> "This is the hag, when maids lie on their backs,
> that presses them and learns them first to bear,
> making them women of good carriage."

To be 'hag-ridden' was to suffer nightmares and 'the hagge' was conceived to be a hideous witch or succubus who sat on a sleeper's stomach and caused bad dreams. For example, in the *Mad pranks and merry jests of Robin Goodfellow,*[132] Gull the Fairy describes how "Many times I get on men and women and so lie on their stomachs that I cause them great pain; for which they call me by the name of Hagge and Nightmare." The victim's experience is that

> "the nightmare hath prest,
> With that weight on their breast,
> No returnes of their breath can pass."[133]

In Drayton's *Nymphidia* this sensual nature of this sensation is addressed more explicitly:

---

131   *The Cozenages of the Wests,* 1613.
132   1588, Percy Society, 1841, p.42.
133   *The Holly Bush,* 1646.

"And Mab, his merry queen, by night,
Bestrides young folk that lie up-right,
(in older times the mare that hight.)"

This notion is then transformed by Shakespeare into something akin to an incubus not only seducing – but even educating – virgin girls.

CHAPTER NINE

Goblin Market

THE FAIRY ECONOMY

"Come buy our orchard fruits,
Come buy, come buy."
Goblin Market, Christina Rossetti.

Faery was believed in many respects to mirror human society: brownies undertook house work, farm labour and other domestic chores like sewing, whilst the 'trooping fairies' and pixies had their own king and queen, a royal court, dances and hunts. These parallels extended to holding and frequenting fairs and markets.

On one hand, this mirroring of human commerce seems incongruous: one very notorious fairy trait was to steal human food products (or, at least) the nourishment within them. In his *Secret commonwealth* Robert Kirk described how the fairies fed on "the Foyson or substance of Corns and Liquors or corn itself that grows on the Surface of the Earth." As a result, he said, "When we have plenty, they have Scarcity at their Homes" meaning that "We then ... do labour for that abstruse People, as weill as for ourselves."[134] Milk from which the goodness has been extracted floats like a cork on water, he alleged. In the traditional Scottish ballad *Young Tamlane* the hero of the title declares that "all our wants are well supplied, From every rich man's store." The fairies' thieving is openly confessed, albeit with a Robin Hood style justification. All the same, it may be understandable why one poet denounced the "sluggish, lazy, thriftlesse elves..."[135]

---

134 Kirk, sections 2 & 3 respectively.
135 William Browne, *The Shepherd's Pipe*.

The fairies stole products by a variety of methods:

- *in a hazel switch* (for milk);
- *by stealthy theft* – corn, Kirk said, "these Fairies steal away, partly invisible, partly preying on the Grain as do Crowes and Mice." A granary may be emptied, grain by grain;
- *by ropes* – "What Food they extract from us is conveyed to their Homes by Secret Paths, as sume skilfull Women do the Pith and Milk from their Neighbours Cows into their own Cheife-hold thorow a Hair-tedder, at a great distance, by Airt Magic…;"[136]
- *by a magic chain* – in Argyll it was said that, on a moonlit night, the fairies would fish an enchanted chain from a pool beneath a waterfall. This chain was dragged through the meadows where the cattle grazed, after which all the milk would go to them;[137]
- *by leaving a stock* in place of a stolen cow (as in the story *The Tacksman of Auchriachan*) or by leaving an old man rolled in a cow skin; and,
- *by thieving from market stalls.* The fairies are sometimes encountered in a market place, invisible to all but the person who has touched fairy ointment on an eye and who thereby is no longer fooled by fairy glamour. The punishment for observing the fairies at their work is loss of sight in the eye affected.

Fairy folk can be shameless and open about their thefts. Larceny is a major source of entertainment as well as material supplies. In Randolph's play *Amyntas* the elves sing that:

"Stolen sweets are always sweeter,
Stolen kisses much completer,
Stolen looks are nice in chapels,
Stolen, stolen are your apples.

When to bed the world are bobbing,
Then's the time for orchard robbing;

---

136 Kirk c.3.
137 Campbell, *Popular Tales of the West Highlands*, vol.2, 1890, p.80.

Yet the fruit were scarce worth peeling
Were it not for stealing, stealing."[138]

The fairies are not to be dissuaded from these habits, because "Fairies, like nymphs with child, must have the things they long for." Accordingly, they pilfer dairy products, fruit and anything else that takes their fancies. For instance, if they find people at a feast, they may adopt a disguise to scare off the revellers just so that they may get their hands on the dainties.[139] It might reasonably be proposed that this trait is a fundamental characteristic of fairy kind: "Elves, urchins, goblins all and little fairies that do filch."

Nonetheless, fairies are also said to indulge in labour and trade just like humans. One Welsh tale reports them mowing, herding and mining, just like their human neighbours. Kirk also states that the industrious *sidh* women spin, dye, weave and embroider and that they bake bread and strike hammers in their hills. In the Highlands they are reputed to labour "like tinkers" and, if discovered by a craftsman working with the tools of his trade, can even be compelled to enter into an arrangement called *ceaird chomuinn* (association craft) whereby they will assist in the work whenever required to.[140] These are just other instances of the close parallels between our society and theirs. Fairies are often presented as participating enthusiastically in commerce. The famous fairy fair on the Blackdown Hills featured pewterers, pedlars and fruit and ale sellers.[141] Other well-known fairs were held by the pixies near Breage and at St Germoe in Cornwall.[142] The fairies were said to attend markets and fairs all over Wales and to pay good prices for the wares (though sometimes they were spotted stealing, too). The Welsh also noted the skill of fairies in spinning, weaving, mining and cobbling. As well as organising their own markets, the fairy folk living on islands off the Pembroke and Carmarthen coast (the *Plant Rhys Dwfn*) regularly visited the markets at Laugharne and Milford Haven, at which they always paid the exact price and never spoke to the stall holders.[143]

---

138   Act III, scene 4.
139   *Robin Goodfellow's merry pranks.*
140   Campbell, *Superstitions of the Highlands & Islands*, c.1.
141   Keightley, *Fairy mythology* pp.294-5.
142   Wentz p.171.
143   Sikes pp.9 and 10.

Another Welsh informant observed that the fairies' chatter at night always peaked when the prices were high at Llangefni market.[144]

If one is polite and respectful, it is even possible for humans to trade with the fairies at their own markets. This amenability to a human presence is rare though – normally the intrusion is resented. Ruth Tongue heard such an account in Somerset, the most interesting aspect of which is that change given in dry leaves became gold and silver at home the next day – contrary to the normal nature of fairy 'gold'; more typical is the story told of innkeepers being paid in coins which turned out to be pieces of horn or leather.[145]

In Christina Rossetti's imagining the market was used as a way of luring in innocent humans and as such is another version of the abduction theme in fairy lore. It is however anomalous to the authentic tradition of fairy markets, though, and in truth *Goblin Market* is a product of literature rather than folk imagination. In the poem, Jeanie had tasted the goblins' fruits and thereafter:

> "pined and pined away
> Sought them by night and day,
> Found them no more but dwindled and grew grey."

Some folk tales certainly indicate that fairies possess their own independent wealth, in the form of gold, silver and cattle, though it must be conceded that this may originally have been stolen from humans, as pilfering was consistently reported to be a key element in the elvish economy.[146] Fairies are, therefore, known to pay quite properly for items and services rendered. In one story they feed a pregnant sow and, when she has farrowed, take the piglets but leave money in their place.[147] An odd account from Wales records the fairly common practice of fairies leaving gold in return for water left out by humans – except in this case the coins were said to be of unknown provenance, not British currency but unfamiliar pieces marked with a harp on one side.[148]

---

144   Wentz p.139.
145   *County folklore – Somerset*, vol.8, p.112; Heywood, *The Hierarchie of Blessed Angels*.
146   Wentz pp.106. 144, 147 & 151.
147   *A Pleasant Treatise of Witches*, 1634.
148   John Rhys, *Celtic Folklore* p.6.

Around Bangor it was said that the *Tylwyth Teg* "have plenty of money at their command, which they could bestow on people whom they liked."[149] They would reward those whose behaviour gained their favour (see above and chapter 25 later). A further curious detail concerning the commercial and capitalist nature of faery comes from the *Robin Goodfellow, his mad pranks and merry jests,* in which we are informed that the fairies would lend money to the poor to assist them – and this without interest.

> "For the use demand we nought,
> Our own is all we desire."[150]

This sounds like some sort of social finance, but if they did not pay on the due date, the borrowers would be pinched or punished "in their goods, so that they never thrive til they have paid us."

Despite all this evidence of a separate fairy economy, there was also a constant theme in folklore of the fair folk being to some degree dependent upon humans for the provision of basic items. Frequently, they might rely upon people to provide them with heated water for bathing; they also seemed to lack various basic domestic items and skills to satisfy which they had to resort to human aid. For example a broken plough or baking 'peel' would have to be repaired by a man and the fairies regularly borrowed kitchen gear from their mortal neighbours. Recompense in the form of food was generally made.[151]

In summary, one's assessment of the balance of the faery economy between booty and barter in large measure will depend upon whether or not you regard them as primarily malign or benign. For earlier generations, it will be obvious that the concept of thieving fairies provided a ready explanation of poor harvests, declining yields and lost or mislaid items. Our 'good neighbours', meanwhile, might be expected to prefer pilfering to purchasing as it involved a great deal less effort to live on the fruits of others' labours; moreover, they were considerably aided in their larceny by their ability to disappear. One final consideration obtrudes itself:

---

149   Wentz p.142.
150   *The Pranks of Puck.*
151   Rhys pp.63, 220, 221, 227, 228, 229 & 241.

according to John Rhys fairies can only count to five, the total fingers on one hand. This greatly limited their numerical skills, plainly, and might incline one more to the belief that theft would be preferred to honest trade...[152]

---

152   *Celtic Folklore* c.VII.

CHAPTER TEN

All the power this charm doth owe

FAIRY MAGIC

Magic and enchantment are integral to the nature of the fairy realm in traditional British folklore, but the actual form of these powers is less often explicitly discussed.[153] This chapter will start to do this. To begin with, 'faerie' and enchantment were widely understood to be identical. A few quotes from medieval and early modern literature will demonstrate this:

"To preve the world, alwey, iwis,
Hit nis but fantum and feiri."[154]
"That thou herdest is fairye."[155]
"This is faiery gold, boy."[156]

Everything pertaining to fairies, therefore, is illusory and enchanted. That accepted, the folklore sources indicate that fairies possess a variety of specific magical powers by which humans may be deceived or confused. The following supernatural abilities are reported:

- *shape-shifting* – fairies have the innate power to change their shapes. However, not all fairies can do this. Some have only two shapes available between which they are able to switch (for

---

153 See Roney-Douglas, *The Faery Faith*, p.3.
154 from Pancoast and Spaeth, *Early English Poems*, 1911, p.134: 'the world is nothing but illusion or deception.'
155 *Romance of Kyng Alisaundre* (1438) Book 6, line 324: spoken after the king hears a dire prophecy pronounced by a stone trough.
156 *Winter's Tale,* Act III, scene 3: in other words, the gold discovered by the characters is really just dried leaves; it is an illusion.

instance between man and horse) but bogies, pucks and the like can choose to appear in whatever form they wish. Puck in *Midsummer Night's Dream* delights in this:[157]

> "I am that merry wanderer of the night.
> I jest to Oberon and make him smile
> When I a fat and bean-fed horse beguile,
> Neighing in likeness of a filly foal:
> And sometime lurk I in a gossip's bowl,
> In very likeness of a roasted crab,
> And when she drinks, against her lips I bob
> And on her wither'd dewlap pour the ale.
> The wisest aunt, telling the saddest tale,
> Sometime for three-foot stool mistaketh me;
> Then slip I from her bum, down topples she,
> And 'tailor' cries, and falls into a cough."

Puck's shape-shifting habits are one of his defining features and are mentioned in the old popular accounts of his 'merry pranks'. He can look like a different person, or appear like an ox, a crow or a snarling hound.[158]

- *the perils of shape-shifting* – in Cornish fairy lore there is an unusual price to pay for the magical ability to change physical form. It is said that every time one of the *Pobel Vean* (the little people) do this, becoming a bird or such like, they get permanently smaller. This continues until they reach a point where they have shrunk to the size of a *muryan* (an ant) and so effectively disappear.
- *vanishing* – controlling their visibility is one of the major fairy attributes (although it is not clear if this is inherent or achieved through the use of magic potions, such as fern seed).[159] This power is widely accepted across Britain, from the Highlands to Cornwall.[160] Interestingly, Bessie Dunlop of Lynn in Ayrshire, on

---

157   Act II, scene 1.
158   *Robin Goodfellow – his mad pranks and merry jests.*
159   See Drayton, *Nymphidia.*
160   Wentz pp.100, 102, 114, 138, 141, 144, 145 & 176.

trial for witchcraft in 1576, stated that the fairies' disappearances were accompanied by a "hideous ugly howling sound, like that of a hurricane." It is possible too to extend this power to humans and make them disappear.[161] The fairies can choose whether and when to reveal themselves to mortals, appearing and disappearing at will: Aubrey informs us that "indeede it is saide they seldom appeare to any persons who go to seeke for them."[162] However, in some circumstances, this power can be overridden by human action. A four leaf clover can give the power to see,[163] as can being in the company of an uneven number of people,[164] looking through a knot hole, application of fairy ointment to the eyes and being born with the 'second sight'. This innate ability could then be communicated to another who was not gifted by mere contact.[165] Invisibility can also be achieved using fern seed, although this can only be seen and collected on St John's Eve according to Sir Walter Scott.[166]

- *glamour* – this is the power of enchantment or disguise in its purest form. How it is imparted is not analysed, but it seems to comprise a spell that disguises the true nature of the enchanted thing or place. The word itself comes either from the Icelandic *glamr,* meaning a ghost or spirit, or instead from the old Scots English *gramarye,* denoting the spell or enchantment that bestows the disguise. As mentioned previously, the application of an ointment to the eyes (usually forbidden and accidental) frequently enables a human to dispel the glamour. This idea is widespread throughout the island of Britain.[167] This ointment invariably has to be applied by a human midwife attending a fairy birth and will be subject to an injunction that the midwife does not anoint herself. Her breach of this will lead to the loss of her sight or at least of her second sight.

161 Wentz p.100.
162 John Aubrey, *Natural History of Wiltshire.*
163 see for example Evans Wentz p.177; Hunt, *Popular Romances.*
164 Sikes p.106.
165 Kirk, section 12; Wentz p.153.
166 *Minstrelsy* Part III.
167 see for example Keightley pp.311-12 or Wentz p.175.

Violation of the glamour in these midwife stories results in harsh retribution, but we will end this paragraph on a more cheerful note. One very particular example of fairy illusion relates to cases where a person is deceived into believing that they have visited a fine house, or inn, or outdoor celebration, and enjoyed feasting, drinking and dancing in good company. These pleasure – filled nights end with the human retiring to sleep in a luxurious bed, only to find themselves out on the open moor in the morning, asleep in a sheepfold or stretched out on the heather or rushes. These adventures are harmless enough, given the all too common risk of being abducted by dancing fairies;

- *elf-shots* – in a later chapter I will describe how fairies can blight and injure by means of arrows and the like (see chapter 20). These wounds and plagues are understood to be inflicted either by physical weapons, with which cursed or charmed missiles are fired, or by more plainly magical means. As just described in the previous paragraph, human helpers to the fairies can sometimes unwittingly penetrate the glamour by smearing a balm on one or both eyes. This violation of the fairies' secrecy is normally punished by blinding – a jab in the eye with a stick; but sometimes a mere puff of breath in the face will have the same effect – a more obviously magical retribution for a magical transgression. The Reverend Kirk expresses it thus:

> "if any Superterraneans be so subtile, as to practice Slights by procuring a Privacy to any of their Misteries, (such as making use of their ointments, which ... makes them invisible, or casts them in a trance, or alters their Shape, or makes Things appear at a vast Distance), they smite them without Paine, as with a Puff of Wind..."[168]

In one case a fairy spitting in a woman's face was sufficient to deprive her of her ability to see through the glamour.[169]

---

168   s.4.
169   Rhys p.248.

- *levitation* – in recent centuries fairies have grown wings that enable them to get around (see chapter 28). Before that, their means of transport was much more obviously magical (see chapter 13). Powers of flight could be imparted to inanimate objects too, so that a building that attracted fairy ire could be moved elsewhere;

- *magical names* – as I discuss in chapter 19, power over a fairy can be gained by possession of his/her concealed name, which in this context becomes a spell in itself; and,

- *allure* – as mentioned in chapter 1 folklore has always ascribed irresistible beauty to fairy women (especially the *gwragedd annwn* of the Welsh lakes). This allure may well be a form of enchantment in itself, giving the fairy power over a weak human.

Pursuing this theme to its logical conclusion, we may finally note the interesting fact that the products of fairy/ human relationships do *not* automatically possess their supernatural parents' abilities. In the pamphlet *Robin Goodfellow, his mad pranks and merry jests,* published in 1628, Robin Goodfellow (*Puck*) is revealed to be a half-human sprite. He needs to be formally granted his father's powers by means of a scroll, although it seems apparent that the potentiality was there from birth, waiting to be released. Once acquired, this power enables Robin to obtain anything he wishes for and to change himself "to horse, to hog, to dog, to ape..."

CHAPTER ELEVEN

Where should this music be? i' the air or the earth?

FAIRY PASTIMES

As has been discussed, the residents of fairyland spend a good deal of their time tormenting humans, either maliciously or mischievously, some in thievery from hapless mortals and a little in honest commerce. The impression gained from folklore though, is that mostly the fairy life was one of leisure, with nothing to do but have fun.

Again and again the sources connect the fairies with pleasure and revelry, and in particular:

- *dancing* appears to have been their chiefest delight and one of their commonest attributes. Frequent references are made to fairies 'tripping,' 'frisking' or to their nimble feet. It might almost be said to be definitive: for example, see *Macbeth* – "Like elves and fairies in a ring."[170] Most often dancing is said to take place at night and in open places. In Cornwall fairies are said to dance at their fairs, although again these are most likely to be held in open spaces.[171] Humans might be lured to join these 'wanton' dances and would have great trouble escaping.
- *"most dainty music"* – music naturally accompanied the dancing, both instrumental and vocal; for example Thomas Brown in *The Shepherd's Pipe* describes fairies dancing to piping in meadows or in fields of yellow box. In Wales they played harps,[172] whilst

---

170 Act IV, scene 1.
171 Wentz p.171.
172 Sikes c.7.

in Scotland the bagpipes appear to have been preferred. John Dunbar of Invereen said that the *sidh* were "awful for the bagpipes" and often were heard playing them.[173] Fairies are frequently associated with particular pipes and chanters in the Highlands and it is also notable that their musical skills might be bestowed upon fortunate humans.[174] Equally, it is said, several folk tunes are originally fairy airs, heard and memorised by attentive players. To human ears the fairy music was invariably found to be 'soft and sweet' and nearly irresistible – especially to younger people.[175] Throughout Shakespeare's *The Tempest* "heavenly music" is a central element to the enchantments used by Prospero and Ariel, lending it a magical as well as pleasurable aspect. Humans, it seems, are welcome to join in fairy songs (just as with dances) so long as they are polite and, possibly even more importantly, musical, so that their contribution is harmonious and positive. Woe betide the poor vocalist: in one Scottish case a hump back who sang well and enhanced a song was rewarded by having his hump taken away; a jealous imitator who tried to repeat this spoiled the rhyme and was punished by bestowal of the hump;[176]

- *feasting* too went along with the enjoyment of song and dance. Banqueting, wine and ale are frequently alluded to (in the Cornish stories of Selena Moor and Miser on the Gump, for instance). A Zennor girl came upon pixy 'junketting' in an orchard near Newlyn.[177] In many of the instances when fairy hills are seen to open up it is to reveal a fine feast within.[178]

- *riding* provided the other major pastime. The *'fairy rade'* or procession features in a large number of stories, for example *Allison Gross* and *Tam Lin*. These processions are described as being richly caparisoned and very stately. Mounted fairies also

---

173   Wentz p.95.
174   Wentz pp.86 & 111& 103.
175   Rhys pp.53, 86, 96 & 111; Wentz p.159.
176   Wentz p.92.
177   Wentz p.175.
178   for example William of Newborough, Book I, c.28 & Keightley p.283.

liked to hunt, although these outings tend to be far noisier and wilder affairs. We are normally never surely told what is was that the fairies preferred to chase, although we often hear of their abandoned gallops across the countryside with their hounds; nevertheless in the poem *Sir Orfeo* we meet "The king off fary and all hys route ... with hundes berkyng;" he is in search of deer.

- *visiting human houses* – many of the activities described so far could take place in fairy hills or out in the open – at fairy rings, standing stones and similar sites; it is evident, though, that fairies would commonly congregate at human homes for their assemblies and entertainments. In the *Merry Pranks of Puck* we are told that "sundry houses did they use" for their revelry and in folk stories from Stowmarket and from Penwith we hear of fairies meeting in houses for their own purposes. Over and above this imposition, they might cause a nuisance, their last entertainment;

- *mischief* might fairly be said to be a fairy entertainment. The taunting of humans was a primary source of pleasure for several types of fairy – especially the pucks and hobgoblins, and this is exemplified by Thomas Heywood in his *Hierarchie of the Blessed Angels* when he describes how they enjoy gambolling at night on a household's shelves and settles, making a noise with the pots and pans and waking up the sleeping inhabitants.[179]

In all of the above, it will be noted, the fairies mirrored the activities of earthly royal courts and noble houses. At the end of *Midsummer Night's Dream,* for example, we are told that Oberon in Theseus' palace "doth keep his revels here tonight." Overall, in fact, the strong impression gained from a study of the accounts (both traditional and literary) is that the fairies' time was mainly filled with pleasure and mischief, and that there was only a very a scanty 'work ethic.' This is echoed in a comment on the Anglesey fairies: a woman observed with some disapproval that "all the good they ever did was singing and dancing."[180]

---

179   1636, p.574.
180   Wentz p.139.

CHAPTER TWELVE

Fairy Ground

THE NATURE AND USE OF FAIRY RINGS

"Come follow, follow me,
You Fairie Elves that be;
And circle round this greene.
Come follow me your Queene.
Hand in hand let's dance a round,
For this place is Fayrie ground."

Dancing, as we have seen, was a defining occupation of the fairies. The activity produced fairy rings, which were similarly characteristic of the supernatural presence, and as such both require our attention.

The fairies danced in a number of locations, but these were always outside and nearly always lushly grassy: Drayton speaks of 'pleasant lawns', for example.[181] The places preferred included:

- on hills, for instance at Sennen near Land's End,[182] or on sloping or rising ground;[183]
- on marshy land – West Country pixies were known to prefer damper ground [184] but they were not alone in this – Welsh fairies for example were often associated with low, rushy spots;[185]
- in grassy fields, pastures or meadows;[186]

---

181 *Nymphal* 10.
182 Wentz p.182.
183 Rhys p.60; Drayton, *Polyolbion* XXI.
184 Wentz p.184.
185 Rhys p.112; Drayton, *Nymphidia* and *Shepherd's Sirena*.
186 Wentz pp.142, 143, 153 & 155; Jonson, *Tale of a Tub*, II, 1.

- in dry places, preferentially under oak trees; there they leave reddish circles – most often under the female oaks.[187]

These dances took place at night (like much fairy activity) and more especially in moonlight.[188] The fondness for moonlight is a widespread preference recorded in literature, including Milton in *Comus* – "Now to the moon in wavering morrice move...",[189] and, of course, Shakespeare, who mentions 'moonshine revels' in both *Midsummer Night's Dream* and *The Merry Wives of Windsor*.[190] The dancing itself was invariably a circle dance, the music for these "quick measures" being provided on the pipes by goblin Tom Thumb.[191] The music and the 'graceful and attractive' dances were nearly always irresistible to humans.[192]

If the night was dark, a glow worm might supply illumination at the centre of the 'nightly rounds.'[193] Alternatively, as in one late nineteenth century case on the Isle of Skye, the fairies tripped around a bonfire.[194]

"Round about, round about, in a fine ring-a,
Thus we dance, thus we dance, and this we sing-a,
Trip and go, to and fro, over this green-a,
All about, in and out, for our brave queen-a."[195]

The effect of these 'ringlets' was to leave a distinct mark on the grass. Generally called fairy rings, they were also known as 'hag tracks' in Sussex and as 'pisky beds' in the South West. A number of explanations and descriptions exist. The tell-tale sign of fairy dancing was a circle of noticeably greener grass on the turf,[196] but the ring might be red and bare of grass [197] or might be formed of mushrooms, for which reason

187   Wentz p.106.
188   Wentz pp.84, 142, 159, 181; Scott, *Minstrelsy*; Rhys p.83; Fletcher, *The Faithful Shepherdess*, I, 2; Drayton, *Shepherd's Sirena*.
189   lines 115-117.
190   Shakespeare, Act II scene 2 and Act V scene 5 respectively.
191   *Robin Goodfellow, his mad pranks*.
192   Rhys p.53.
193   Rhys p.60.
194   See Briggs, *Fairies in Tradition* p.20.
195   Lyly, *The Maydes Metamorphosis*, II, 1.
196   Rhys p.176.
197   Rhys p.245 & Wentz p.106.

Prospero in *The Tempest* addresses elves as "you whose pastime/ Is to make midnight mushrooms."[198] Sir Walter Scott recorded that Scottish fairies would dance on conical hills "by moonlight, impressing upon the surface the mark of circles, which sometimes appear yellow and blasted, sometimes a deep green hue." Robert Burton observed that fairies danced on heaths and greens and "leave that green circle which we commonly find in plain fields, which others hold to proceed from a meteor falling, or some accidental rankness of the ground, so nature sports herself."[199] Scott noted too that lumps of turf scooped out of the ground by lightning strikes were blamed on the fairies. Fairy rings are mentioned by Prospero in *The Tempest* who invokes "Ye elves ... that/ By moonshine do the green-sour ringlets make/ Whereof the ewe not bites."[200] Finally, the tracks might be seen in snow as well as on grass.[201]

Fairy rings were more than a curiosity and a hint of hidden mysteries. They were regarded as perilous. Scott warned that it was dangerous to sleep in one or to remain there after sunset. The least punishment might be the usual pinching (see chapter 20),[202] but it could prove impossible to escape from the dance without a determined rescuer to help.[203] There was a well-known fairy ring at Brington, Northamptonshire, of which it was said that, if a person ran round nine times at full moon, they would hear mirth and revelry underground but would have fallen into the fairies' power. The same was said of a ring near Alnwick.[204]

I shall conclude with a quotation from *Britannia's Pastorals* by William Browne, in which all the principal features of rings are neatly summarised:

"Near to this wood there lay a pleasant mead,
Where fairies often did their measures tread.
Which in the meadow made such circles green,
As if with garlands it had crowned been,

---

198 Wentz pp.182 & 173; *Round about our Coal Fire*,1734, c.VI; Shakespeare, *The Tempest*, V,1.
199 *The Anatomy of Melancholy*, p.124.
200 Act V, scene 1.
201 Halliwell XXXIII.
202 Haliwell XVIII.
203 Rhys pp.176, 200 & 239.
204 Keightley p.310.

Or like the circle where the signs we track,
And learned shepherds call't the Zodiac :
Within one of these rounds was to be seen
A hillock rise, where oft the fairy-queen
At twilight sat, and did command her elves..."[205]

---

205   Book I, song 2, lines 389-404.

CHAPTER THIRTEEN

In the church-path way to glide

FAIRY TRAVEL

How do fairies get about? Fluttering wings are a relatively recent attribute (see chapter 28). Before this development, the fair folk relied upon quite prosaic means:

- they are known to walk in procession along the highways like any mortal;[206] or,
- more often, they will ride. As is known, the fairies are hunters and keep steeds for this purpose. Welsh fairies, it was said, were very fond of going on horseback and rode small white horses that did not touch the ground.[207] Cromek described steeds "whose hoof would not print the new ploughed land or dash the dew from the crop of a harebell."[208] The so-called trooping fairies got their name as a result of their habit of riding around in great state, their greatest procession being at Roodmass eve.

In this connection, there is a little evidence in Britain of what are called fairy paths (or roads or avenues). Wentz mentions evidence from Carmarthenshire of *tylwyth teg* paths. These are, he says, "precisely like those reserved for the Irish good people or for the Breton dead ... it is death to a mortal while walking in one of these paths to meet the *tylwyth teg*."[209] From the West of England there are recollections of 'trods', straight

---

206 Sikes 107; Rhys 272, 277 & 279.
207 Sikes 107.
208 Cromek, Appendix F.
209 Wentz 150. Sadly he does not give the full story told to his informant, but he does however give details of Irish and Breton belief: pp.33, 38, 67, 77, 218, 231 & 277.

lines of greener grass across fields where cattle will not graze. A person may be cured of rheumatism by walking the trod, but it would be dangerous to meet a supernatural procession coming the other way. These paths or passes are akin to ley lines and corpse roads, it would seem. They link sites of traditional significance (standing stones, barrows, rocks and trees) in straight lines. The fairies glided along just above the tracks, not liking to deviate,[210] and those who built on or obstructed their routes met with their displeasure. The only options then were to demolish and rebuild elsewhere, or to leave doors and windows open at night so that the fairies could pass straight through. One witness observed the fairies of Nithsdale going straight through a hedge and across a corn field to their destination without leaving a trace on the crops.[211]

The foregoing problems might all seem rather puzzling given the fairies' known ability to fly (albeit not conventionally with wings). Their means of transport was magical: for example, according to Reginald Scot, "hempen stalks" plucked in the fields would be used as horses.[212] The fairies could also travel about on ragwort stems, on beans or in whirling clouds of dust, using a spoken hex to get themselves airborne.[213] In one Scottish account they got airborne by saying "My king at my head/ Going across in my haste/ On the crests of the waves/ To Ireland."[214] John Aubrey gives a much simpler spell, "Horse and hattock", and examples in between are also quite common.[215] Travel in whirls of dust, especially on days that were otherwise still, was so distinctive as to be known as 'the people's puff of wind' in the Highlands.[216]

210 *Fireside Stories of Ireland,* P. Kennedy, Dublin, 1870.

211 Keightely p.355.

212 *Discoverie of Witchcraft* Book II c.4.

213 Keightley p.290; Evans Wentz p.87 & see too p.152 – the *Tylwyth Teg* can move or fly about at will.

214 Wentz p.87.

215 Aubrey, *Miscellanies;* Briggs, *Dictionary,* 'Fairy Levitation.'

216 Campbell, *Popular Superstitions of the Highlands & Islands,* c.1.

Cautionary tales

THE SOCIAL FUNCTION OF FAIRIES

In his book *Religion and the Decline of Magic* Keith Thomas astutely observed that "Fairy faith has a social function, enforcing certain conduct" and that "Fairy beliefs could help to reinforce some of the standards upon which the effective working of society depended."[217] There were two main targets for these warnings – children and servants/ wives. The two groups shared subordinate social positions and could be the subject of rebukes and punishments. One vehicle for such chastisement was supernatural.

Then, as now, children from time to time needed to be told what was best for them. A fairy threat to enforce this, especially in situations when adults might be absent, was a valuable support to parents. A variety of risks and dangers were given fairy personality in the hope of instilling an awed respect and nervous caution. The perils given terrifying character included:

- *rivers* – for example 'Peg Powler' on the river Tees, who might drag incautious children from the banks under the waves;
- *ponds* – similar dangers, as well as that of lawn-like mats of pond weed, were given identities: Jenny Greenteeth in Lancashire and Cumbria, Grindylow in Yorkshire, Nelly Longarms and the widespread Rawhead and Bloodybones. In East Anglia the 'freshwater mermaid' was especially well known. There are records of these perilous creatures in the River Gipping in Suffolk and in ponds, pools and meres at Fordham, Cambridgeshire and in Suffolk at Rendlesham and at the Mermaid Pits, Fornham All

---

217   pp.730 and 732.

Saints. The fearsome sprite of inland waters is an ancient English dread. Layamon's *Brut* of around 1205 described a Scottish lake: "nikers bathe therein; there is the play of elves in the hideous pool;"[218]

- *unripe fruit in trees* – to discourage theft and upset stomachs, infants were warned of Awd Goggie, Lazy Lawrence and the Colt Pixy in orchards; Churnmilk Peg and Melsh Dick guarded Yorkshire nut groves and the Gooseberry Wife, in the form of a huge caterpillar, lay in wait amidst the fruit bushes on the Isle of Wight;

- *domestic store rooms* – dangers in the home were protected by Tom Poker in Suffolk and Bloody Bones elsewhere.

Bogies also had the function of getting children to behave themselves and to go to bed. Amongst these so-called nursery bogies were Tankerabogus, Mumpoker and Tom Dockin.

Adults undertaking domestic duties would be chastened by fairy retribution too. The so-called 'buttery sprites' existed as the grownup equivalent to the creatures deployed to terrify children. A range of chores were policed by supernatural means. This theme is comprehensively summarised in the *Fairies Fegaries* of 1635:

"And if the house be foule
Or platter, dishe or bowle
Upstairs we nimbly creepe
And finde the sluts asleepe:
Then we pinch their arms and thighs
None escapes nor none espies.
But if the house be swepte
And from uncleanesse kept
We praise the house and maid
And surely she is paid:
For we do use before we go
To drop a tester in her shoe."

218   Brut ix.

Servants were warned not to sit up late gossiping but to keep their houses tidy, floors and hearths swept and the embers raked up, dairies spotless, the shelves dusted, the benches wiped down and their pewter well scoured. Those "foul sluts" who neglected their chores did so on pain of physical punishment: they would be pinched black and blue all over, whilst the obedient and dutiful would be rewarded with a coin in a shoe or pail.[219] Neglect of the proper domestic offerings to fairies – clean water, milk, bread and the like – led to infliction of the same penalties.

In summary then, fairy lore was not just a source of entertainment or explanation of puzzling events; they had a regulatory function, providing invisible, semi-divine supervision of the activities of some members of society.

---

219   see for example Thomas Churchyard, *A Handful of Gladsome Verses*, 1592 or William Browne, *Britannia's Pastorals*, Book 1, song 2.

CHAPTER FIFTEEN

Of Brownyis and of Boggles, full is this beuk

THE HELPFUL FAIRIES

"And then outspoke a brownie,
With a long beard on his chin:
'I spun up all the tow' said he,
'And I want some more to spin.'"[220]

For all that has been said about the divine, fearsome and sometimes vengeful nature of British fairies, I have mentioned – and many readers will be familiar with – a species of helpful household beings. This category of supernaturals is often labelled 'brownies' but this is one regional variation (of eastern and northern England and the Scottish Lowlands) of a wider class which, as the above quote from Gawain Douglas indicates, includes the hobgoblins, hobs and lobs. There are also those fairies that are made useful to humans by reason of scaring recalcitrant children (Tom Dockin, Tom Poker, Tommy Rawhead *et al*) – see the previous chapter on these nursery sprites. Here we are concerned with those beings that render aid voluntarily and devotedly.

These solitary fairies were more or less domesticated, being attached to a family or place. One manuscript source explains that hobgoblins and Robin Goodfellows are:

"more familiar and domestical then the others, and for some causes to us unknown, abode in one place more then in another, so that

---

220 *The Fairies of Caldon-low,* Mary Howitt.

some never almost depart from some particular houses, as though they were their proper mansions."[221]

These various spirits were all linked with human habitations and human activities, but the degree of association varied. There were, for example:

- *herding fairies* like the Highland *urisk* who cared for cattle and worked in the fields, but lived in or near pools. Some herded sheep or looked after poultry and the Cornish Browney gathered up bee swarms;

- *barn and household fairies* which included the likes of Robin Roundcap of East Yorkshire; Dobie, Dobby and Master Dobbs of the Borders, Northern England and Sussex respectively; the Welsh *bwca* and *bwbachod*; the *bodachan sabhail* of the Highlands, and Old Man Crook and John Tucker of Devon. These fairies would undertake a huge variety of sometimes arduous tasks; they would fan grain, stamp flax seeds, break and dress hemp, spin tow, grind malt and flour, mow, churn, card wool, sweep and wash, riddle corn and boult meal in the pantry, thresh, run errands (such as fetching a midwife) and give advice – or they would untidy that which was already tidy! There was a saying 'Master Dobbs has been helping you' meaning that a person had done more work than had been expected of them; it was believed that brownies could work twice as fast as mortals. It was a key element of the belief that the brownies would labour excessively. See for example Milton's *L'Allegro*:

  > "When in one night, ere glimpse of morn,
  > His shadowy flail hath thresh'd the corn
  > That ten day-labourers could not end";

- *buttery sprites and cellar ghosts* who guard larders from thieving servants. For example, one text describes the ubiquitous Robin Goodfellow as one of the "pleasantly disposed ... spirits ... of the buttery";[222]

---

221 MS Harl. 6482.
222 *Tarlton's Newes out of Purgatorie*, 1590.

- *housework helpers* like Habetrot and Scantlie Mab who assisted with spinning and weaving; and,
- *mine fairies* – Milton knew of "the swart faery of the mine" by which he meant the knockers and *coblynau* who help and guide miners to the best lodes.[223]

Most of these creatures were small and hairy, perhaps at most clad in rags. They were the archetype of Ben Jonson's "Coarse and country fairy,/ That doth haunt the hearth and dairy."[224] They worked hard and energetically and expected no direct reward except some clean water, cream, honeycomb or bread left out before the fire, discretely and without announcement.

Any attempt to give clothes (or at least cheap clothes) by way of recompense for their labours was never appreciated and could either drive a brownie away or convert it into a boggart, a nuisance brownie who behaved like a poltergeist with mischievous tricks. An example from North Wales tells of a fairy at a farm in the Pennant valley who assisted with putting the children to bed. The farmer's wife appreciated this and, pitying the fairy's rags, made her a new gown – which was ripped to shreds in response.[225] Brownies reacted the same way to criticism of their work or if their name was discovered (or if an unwanted human name was given).[226]

Sometimes, brownies could become too attached and too devoted to households. In Ben Jonson's *The Silent Woman* Dauphine complains that "they haunt me like fairies and give me jewels here; I cannot be rid of them."[227] This might seem inexplicable were it not for a Cardiganshire belief that:

"once you come across one of the fairies you cannot easily be rid of him, since the fairies were little beings of a very devoted nature. Once a man had become friendly with one of them, the latter would

---

223 see for example Ritson pp.37-38 *Dissertation on Fairies.*
224 *Masque of Oberon,* 1610.
225 Rhys p.109.
226 see Briggs, *Tradition and Literature* p.34.
227 Act V scene 1.

be present with him almost everywhere he went, until it became a burden to him."[228]

They might then overstep the mark, stealing from neighbouring farms to supply their own. Sometimes they exposed lazy servants, but equally they might defend them, as in a case where the brownie left until servants dismissed for laziness by letting him do all the work were reinstated.[229]

Boggarts and brownies could become such a nuisance to households that a farmer might decide to 'flit' to try to escape from one. There are widespread versions of this tale in Lincolnshire, Yorkshire and Northumberland. The decision might be made to move house; the contents would be packed and loaded and the family would set off, only to find that the brownie was in the cart and was moving with them – so they might as well turn round and stay put, of course.[230]

Finally, we should note that Brownies are now junior girl-guides. The name was taken from Juliana Horatia Ewing's story of *The Brownies* (1870), in which two children learn that they can be either helpful brownies or lazy boggarts. Originally Baden-Powell had chosen the name of 'Rosebuds', so perhaps it was wisely replaced.

Spirits related to those described here are those that warn humans of danger, such as the Cornish hopper and the Isle of Man *houlaa*, who both alerted fishermen to approaching storms and the skriker of Yorkshire and Lancashire who warned of impending death.

---

228 Rhys *Celtic Folklore* p.250.
229 Briggs, *Tradition and Literature* p.38.
230 See Keightley pp.307-8 or Sikes p.117.

CHAPTER SIXTEEN

With each a little changeling in their arms

FAIRY THEFTS OF CHILDREN

"Some night tripping fairy had exchanged,
In cradle clothes our children where they lay..."[231]

I have several times alluded to the very widespread problem of changelings, but I want to examine it more closely in this chapter. It was an article of the fairy faith throughout the British Isles that our 'good neighbours' were not averse to snatching human infants if the opportunity presented itself. The fairy queen herself, is accused of this crime by Ben Jonson:

"This is she that empties cradles,
Takes out children, puts in ladles."[232]

The fairies preferred infants with fair hair and pale skin and took only boys.[233] We may recall the child over whom Titania and Oberon squabble in *A Midsummer Night's Dream*. The queen has newly acquired a servant, "A lovely boy, stolen from an Indian king; She never had so sweet a changeling." Oberon wants the youth as his 'henchman,' as a 'knight in his train' but Titania will not release him.[234]

In place of the stolen human child was left the 'changeling', a creature consistently identifiable because it looked like an old man – being ugly, deformed, small, weak and bad-tempered. Whatever care it received, the

---

231 Shakespeare, *Henry IV Part One*, Act I, scene 1.
232 *Entertainment at Althorpe*, 1603.
233 Rhys p.221; Wentz p.148.
234 Act II, scene 1.

substitute remained frail and did not grow, being peevish at all times. In other words, in earlier times before medical knowledge had developed, if a new-born was discovered to be mentally disabled or defective, this was put down not to congenital or perinatal problems but to a supernatural intervention: the real child had been abducted and an 'oaf' (an elf) left in its place (the 'ouphs' of Shakespeare's *Merry Wives of Windsor* are derived from the same source). Drayton in *Nymphidia* summarises the state of sixteenth century popular belief on paediatrics:

> "...when a child haps to be got
> Which after proves an idiot
> When folke perceive it thriveth not
> The fault therein to smother
> Some silly doting brainless caulf
> That understands things by the half
> Say that the fairy left this aulf
> And took away the other."[235]

We may also note mention from Wales of a belief that the fairies might pay mortals to steal suitable children for them. From South Wales comes the story of an old woman from Cwm Tawe who was believed in her neighbourhood to abduct healthy babes and replace them with old urchins in return for fairy gold.[236] She would enter homes begging for alms and then offer to rock the cradle. Whilst the mother's back was turned, the fairy whelp hidden beneath her cloak would hastily be swapped for the healthy child and the crone would make her escape.

The stolen children seemed generally to be well cared for and to enjoy life at the fairy court, spending their time in feasting, dancing and music. The Cornish story of Betty Stogs tends to support this.[237] Hunt said in the 'high countries' of Penwith (Morva, Zennor and Towednack) that the fairies would take poorly cared for children and clean them. This was Stogs' experience – she neglected her home and her child but the pixies removed the infant, washed its clothes and left it near the cottage

---

235   *The Court of Fairy.*
236   Rhys p.255.
237   Hunt, *Popular Romances of the West of England.*

covered in flowers. Similar accounts are given of Highland fairies.[238]

There is, too, a little evidence that the fairies sought to make their captives immortal like themselves. In one play we are told how the elves danced at a well by–

> "pale moonshine, dipping often times
> Their stolen children, so to make them free
> From dying flesh and dull mortality."[239]

These lines could very well be linked to some verse of Ben Jonson, who in the *Sad Shepherd* recounted a story of:

> "... span long elves that dance about a pool,
> With each a little changeling in their arms!"

This belief also may go some way to explain an odd account from Wales of a suspected changeling that had to be dipped daily for three months in a cold spring, the result of which was that it thrived, growing 'as fast as a gosling.'[240]

The theft of healthy normal babies and their replacement by an aged elf or a defective fairy infant was perceived to be a very common problem, then, and parents had to guard against it. Children were especially vulnerable in the time before they were baptised and a variety of protective measures were deployed. These included placing bindweed or iron (for example tongs or shears) around the cradle, the burning of leather in the room or the administering to the baby of either milk from a cow grazed on pearl-wort or water in which had been steeped cinders from a fire over which the child had been passed.[241] Another protective was to weave wreaths from oak and ivy withies at the full moon in March.[242] These were kept for a year and any children showing signs of consumption would be passed thrice through the hoops, thereby ensuring them against further supernatural assaults.

If despite all the efforts, a substitution was made, all was not necessarily

---

238 Campbell, *Superstitions of the Highlands and Islands of Scotland*, c.1.
239 Fletcher, *The Faithful Shepherdess* Act I, Scene 2.
240 Rhys p.256.
241 Wentz pp.87 & 91.
242 Sir Walter Scott, *Borders Minstrelsy*.

lost. The parents, once the presence of a changeling had been realised, had to take steps to expose the substitute. If it was an aged fairy, some trick would be performed to get it to reveal itself, by provoking its curiosity. It would exclaim that it had seen oaks grow from acorns and chickens from eggs, but it had never seen beer brewed in an egg shell (or pasties for the reapers mixed in a shell). Sometimes the preternatural knowledge of the changeling might be exposed by chance: in one Highland case the 'sibhreach' child was seen to leap from its cradle to play the bagpipes when the parents were away.[243]

There were several other means of expelling a changeling. Salt might be burned as a magical means of repelling it or a shovel might be heated and held before its face. Magic was resorted to: the Cornish used a four leafed clover placed upon the 'winickey' impostor to recover the abducted baby and from Wales we learn of a curious ritual involving a hen: the mother had to find a black hen without a single white feather and had to kill it; then every window and door in the home except one would be sealed and the whole hen would be set before a wood fire to bake. At the point that all its feathers fell off, the crimbil child would leave and the rightful infant would have been returned.[244]

If these attempts did not succeed and an infant elf was still suspected, far worse treatment could follow, typically placing the baby on a shovel over the fire – but throwing the child directly onto the coals or into a river, ducking it in cold water daily, beating it, bathing it in a solution of foxglove leaves, neglecting its needs, throwing pieces of iron at it or, lastly, placing it outside at night on a dunghill or on the beach as the tide came in, might also be tried.[245] The idea was that the changeling's cries would summon the fairy parents who would save their child and return the stolen human infant. Wirt Sikes in British Goblins discussed the Welsh tradition of the plentyn newid (the new child) and remarked disapprovingly upon the cruelties from time to time inflicted as a result of this changeling belief.[246]

---

243   Wentz p.111.
244   Rhys p.263.
245   Wentz pp.111, 146, 171 & 177; Sikes c.V; Keightley p.356.
246   c.5.

Some parents, however, accepted the 'changeling' as their own and cared for the disabled neonate just as much as they would be expected to do for a healthy baby. I have mentioned before how a mother who behaved in this manner was rewarded financially by the fairies during the infant's life. Another example comes from a Scottish witch trial. John Ferguson approached Jonit Andirson for advice on his '*shag-bairn*', a child the family suspected of being a changeling. Andirson confirmed their diagnosis and advised that she could not retrieve their baby from the fairies; however, if they cared for the changeling as their own, 'they would not want.' In one instance from Devon, a Tavistock woman cared so well for the changeling that the gratified fairies even returned her baby to her.[247]

---

247   Keightley p.300.

CHAPTER SEVENTEEN

Tempters of the Night

WHEN BEST TO ENCOUNTER FAIRIES

Some times of day are better than others for seeing fairies. This is the case for several reasons: some hours are more inherently magical; at certain times of day the light conditions are simply more favourable; and, lastly, fairies themselves prefer certain times to others.

Firstly, Dorset healer John Walsh, who was examined in 1563 on suspicion of witchcraft, said that he met with the fairies between twelve and one noon or at midnight. These hours have been identified as 'liminal' times when the two worlds of faery and humans are not so separate.[248] Notably, numerous Dorset *tumuli* are known as 'music barrows' where, if you sit at midday, you will be able to hear fairy music within. For similar reasons, probably, it was felt that Fridays were an auspicious day for supernatural encounters – especially the evenings.[249]

Secondly, there may be a simple physical explanation for the link with dusk and dark. The Reverend Kirk, in the opening chapter of his *Secret Commonwealth*, informs us that fairies have:

> "light changeable Bodies (like those called Astral), somewhat of the Nature of a condensed Cloud and best seen in Twilight."

Later he described these "chamaeleon like" creatures as being formed of "congealed air." A belief in the crepuscular or nocturnal appearance of fairies was widespread. Informants interviewed in Scotland, Wales and Cornwall in the late nineteenth century consistently gave evidence that elves and

---

248   Rosen, *Witchcraft in England 1558-1618.*
249   Sikes p.105.

pixies were to be seen at dusk or dawn,[250] after darkness had fallen [251] and in moonlight – when they danced (and see chapter 12).[252] It may simply be that, in bright sunlight, we were felt to be less aware of the fairy presence.

Thirdly, and most usually, fairies are found abroad at night. As Prospero says, elves "rejoice to hear the solemn curfew."[253] Night seems to be preferred for three main reasons: because humans are not around, because it is the most suitable time for magic and mischief or because it is most suited to fairy pleasures.

Although humans seem to dread what fairies do at night, they themselves see the dark hours more benignly. They are hidden safely from human eyes and can enjoy themselves – "Their rest, when weary, mortals take/ And none but only fairies wake." John Clare said the same: "Fairies now, no doubt, unseen/ In silent revels sup."[254] During the night hours the fairies enjoy their 'night sports' and revels, unperturbed by the fact that only bats and owls are about. Additionally, we should note the traditional association between brownies and their performance of domestic chores for human households during the hours of darkness – typically when the family will be asleep and can neither witness nor disturb their supernatural helpers.

Nowadays we might wish a child a goodnight and hope that they 'sleep tight and that the bed bugs don't bite.' For earlier ages the risks of the hours of darkness and sleep were far more acute and justified much stronger invocations of protection: Robert Herrick's *Bellman* prays that "Mercie secure ye all, and keep/ The Goblin from ye, while ye sleep;" in Shakespeare's *Cymbeline* the character Imogen asks the gods that they "From fairies and the tempters of the night/ Guard me!" Night time is indissolubly linked to the magical realm and activities of fairies. For example, we have *A Midsummer Night's Dream* in which all the mischief of Titania, Oberon and their court occur over a single night. Puck declares that:

---

250 Wentz pp.108, 145, 154, 158 & 180.
251 Wentz pp.139, 143 & 184.
252 Wentz pp.142, 146, 159 & 181.
253 *The Tempest*, Act V, scene 1.
254 John Clare, *At Evening*.

"Now it is the time of night
That the graves, all gaping wide,
Everyone lets forth his spirit
In the churchway paths to glide:
And we fairies, that do run
By the triple Hecate's team
From the presence of the sun
Following darkness like a dream
Now are frolic…"[255]

Soon after this Oberon commands that "Now until the break of day/ Through this house each fairy stray…" Throughout the play the consciousness of the approach of dawn and the limit upon the fairies' powers is stressed. It is only at Christmas, it seems, that the dangers of the darkness are diminished:

"The nights are wholesome, then no planets strike,
No fairy takes or witch hath power to charm…".[256]

What are the reasons for this fundamental association between night and evil-doing? One may simply be a natural and instinctive human aversion to darkness. In the *Rape of Lucrece* Shakespeare invokes "Sable night, mother of dread and fear."[257] In his cultural history, *At Days' Close – a History of Night Time*, Roger Ekirch devotes the first chapter to the 'Terrors of the night', stressing how for earlier generations the nocturnal hours consistently engendered anxieties over the proximity of the devil, the spirits of the dead and fairies. Without sunlight we feel less secure, more vulnerable, more prey to troubled imaginings. This feeling of insecurity is captured in John Clare's verse – "fairy nations now have leave to reign."[258] They should be out at night and humankind should not.

---

255   Act V scene 2.
256   *Hamlet,* Act I, scene 1.
257   line 17.
258   John Clare, *At Night.*

Other poets confirm the close link with night time and fairies' aversion to daylight. Milton in *Ode on the Nativity* describes how "the yellow skirted Fayes/ Fly after the night steeds, leaving their moon loved maze."[259] In *Paradise Lost* too Milton pictures:

"Fairy elves,
Whose midnight revels by a forest side
Or fountain, some belated peasant sees, or dreams he sees,
While overhead the moon
Sits arbitress."[260]

John Lyly in the *Maydes Metamorphosis* of 1600 has the fairies declare "By the moon we sport and play/ With the night begins our day"[261] and Fletcher in the *Faithful Shepherdess* observes too how "The nimble footed fairies dance their rounds/ By the pale moonshine." We can be left in little doubt that, after sunset, the preferred activity of fairy folk is to dance in circles. In the *Merry Wives of Windsor* Dame Quickly addresses her pretend elves thus:

"Fairies black, grey, green and white,
You moon-shine revellers and shades of night…"
"And nightly, meadow fairies, look you sing … in a ring."[262]

Whatever the explanation, poets have always exploited and played with the nocturnal association. In his poem *Oberon's Palace* Robert Herrick imagined Queen Mab to be "moon-tanned" whilst Simon Steward in *A Description of the King and Queen of Fayries* (1635) imagined Oberon setting his horn to his "moone-burnt lippes." John Lyly in *Endimion* called a fairy "the Queen of Stars."

---

259 line 235.
260 line 781.
261 Act II.
262 Act V scene 5.

Section Three

Human Relationships

CHAPTER EIGHTEEN

Sluts are loathsome to the Fairies

THE MORAL CODE FOR HUMANS

Elves and fairies had very clear and strict ideas as to how humans should behave, not only towards the fairies but also to each other. This was enforced with a system of rewards and punishments. As I discussed earlier, to some degree this must be understood as a form of social regulation upon the part of those telling the fairy tales – lazy maids are warned that their arms and thighs will be pinched ("None escapes, nor none espies").[263] Additionally, though this code has its own independent logic as well.

Fairies displayed:

- *an aversion to human untidiness* and a preference for neatness. The popular tale *Robin Goodfellow, his mad pranks and merry jests,* provides us with a clear statement of unacceptable conditions – the fairies will object where a house "is as cleane as a nasty dog's kennel, in one corner bones, in another eg-shells; behind the doore a heap of dust, the dishes under feet and the cat in the cupboard." To breach these standards usually leads to a merciless pinching. For example, Rowland has his Robin Goodfellow "bepinch the lazie queane" and John Marston in *The Mountebank's Mask* of 1618 alludes to the risk that "lustie Doll, maide of the Dairie,/ Chance to be blew-nipt by the fairie." Robert Herrick, in his poem *The Fairies,* succinctly encapsulates the fairy prejudices in their entirety –

---

263   *Fairies Fegaries* p.2.

"If ye will with Mab find grace
Set each Platter in his place:
Rake the fier up, and get
Water in, ere sun be set.
Wash your Pailes and clense your Dairies;
Sluts are loathsome to the Fairies:
Sweep your house: who doth not so,
Mab will pinch her by the toe."

• *resentment of meanness and rudeness* whilst, conversely, generosity and good manners will be rewarded. However, presumption is also disliked. Taking fairy gifts for granted, for example, or disclosing a person's good fortune to others, will invariably lead to the withdrawal of fairy favour and the loss of the benefits they had bestowed. The obligation to be circumspect about the source of one's good luck is reflected in the words of Ben Jonson's *Entertainment at Althorpe.* Fairies presented a gift to the queen but then admonished her -

"Utter not, we implore you
Who did give it, nor wherefore
And whenever you restore
Yourself to us, you shall have more."

Massinger expressed this same warning with greater foreboding in *The Fatal Dowry*:[264] "But not a word of it – 'tis fairies' treasure,/ Which but revealed brings on the blabber's ruin."
• *an esteem for a fair and generous nature,* helpfulness and a preparedness to lend and share and a cheerful disposition on the part of human beings. Such a demeanour was especially important to the fairies, given that they often depended upon people for the loan of tools and utensils or of food, such as flour or meal.[265]

---

264 Act IV, scene 1.
265 Campbell, *Superstitions of the Highlands and Islands of Scotland,* c.1.

- *truthfulness* – honesty and oath keeping are demanded. Robin Goodfellow declares that he loves the honest and only afflicts "knaves and queanes."[266] Telling the truth is esteemed: "We fairies never injure men, Who dare to tell us true" – and they chastise whoever "seeks to steal a lover true."[267] Whilst truthfulness in humans is expected, it does not always appear to be so important to fairies. Still some Welsh elves laid great stress on the importance of good faith,[268] a virtue which the reverend Kirk confirmed: whilst they were liable to swearing and intemperance, he said, they were not subject to the vices of "Hypocracie, Lying and Dissimulations."[269]

- *dislike of untidiness, sloppiness and laziness.* Serving staff will be punished if they sleep when they should be working, if they stay up late, especially if they are gossiping, if they leave doors open, shoes uncleaned, horses unfed or uncombed or if the house is not cleaned as it should be. The punishment fits the crime, so that – for instance – fairies respond by "misplacing things in ill-ordered houses." Personal neglect, such as unkempt hair or going to bed part dressed or unwashed, is also resented.

For poor housekeeping and want of propriety generally, therefore, Robin Goodfellow and the rest "plague[d] both wife and maid."[270] But the fairies also applied strict rules to love affairs and the fairy attitudes to love and lust are, as we might expect from such beings, contradictory and unfair. There is one set of rules for humans and another, laxer set for the fairies.

There are various virtues and qualities that fairies demand of human beings. True love is one of these. Lovers are expected to be devoted and honourable. The use of force is punished, as are attempts to interfere in the course of true love between young couples. Seventeenth century poet John Fletcher warned that if anyone was found "Forcing of a chastity" a horn will be sounded and the fairies all will run to pinch the violator to

---

266 *Robin Goodfellow, his mad pranks.*
267 *Parnell's Fairy Tale;* Halliwell c.XVIII – *Fairy Song III.*
268 Rhys p.159.
269 Kirk c.11.
270 *A Book of Roxburghe Ballads,* 1847, p.35.

the bone until his lustful thoughts are gone.[271] Hobgoblin Puck does the same: he declares "I love true lovers" whilst disliking wanton wives and cuckolders. In one story he uses his magic powers to save a young woman from the unwanted advances of her lecherous uncle, allowing her to marry her young suitor whilst at the same time reforming the old man.[272]

In aid of true love, the fairy queen chastised women who did not take pity on their pining lovers. Elizabethan poet Thomas Campion told how fairies would be sent to pinch the unkind ladies, whilst to those "that will hold watch with love" the fairy queen would bestow beauty and greater adoration. Conversely, "they that have not fed/ On delight amorous/ She vows that they shall lead/ Apes in Avernus" – in other words, they shall suffer sexual frustration.[273]

Shakespeare's *Midsummer Night's Dream* provides the best examples of fairies promoting the virtues of true love. After toying with Titania and Bottom and with the Athenian lovers, fairy king Oberon brings "joy and prosperity" to the triple weddings that crown the play.[274] He blesses the bridal beds, promising true love and constancy to the couples as well as children who shall "ever be fortunate" and free of deformity.[275]

Midsummer Night's Dream ends on this reassuring note; there is marital harmony in both middle earth and Faery and the guarantee of a prosperous future for the newlyweds. However, these gifts come from Oberon, a notoriously unfaithful seducer. When we first meet him in the play, he is accused by his wife Titania of stealing away from fairy land and "versing love/ To amorous Phillida."[276] Worse still, he is revealed elsewhere to be father of Puck after seducing an innocent girl. This is the other side of Faery: high standards are demanded of humans but are not applied to supernaturals.

---

271 *The Faithful Shepherdess*, Act III, scene 1.
272 *Robin Goodfellow, his mad pranks and merry jests.*
273 'Hark all you ladies', in *Astrophel & Stella*, 1591.
274 Act II, scene 1.
275 Respectively Act IV, scene 1 and Act V, scene 2.
276 Act II, scene 1.

In *Oberon's Palace* by Thomas Herrick the fairy king is displayed in the worst possible light. After a feast he goes to Queen Mab's bed ready "For Lust and action." Their chamber is hung about with pearls made from the tears of "ravished Girles/ Or writhing Brides." The music is provided by elves who imitate "the cries/ Of fained-lost Virginities" so as to "excite/ A more unconquered appetite." This is probably the more authentic Faery: it is natural and uninhibited. Oberon was not alone amongst fairy monarchs in his predatory behaviour. Women were often stolen as brides, a good example being in the Middle English poem about *Sir Orfeo* whose wife is enchanted and kidnapped by the king of fairy. Sadly, she was not alone: later folk tales repeat this theme.

Fairy maidens can be as predatory as the men. They can abduct and seduce hapless youths using their renowned beauty and allures. In an early English poem, Round Table knight Launval encounters fairy lady Tryamour. She is found in a pavilion, nearly naked in the heat and lying on a couch – "white as the lily in May/ or snow that snows on a winter's day." Launval is instantly obsessed, and soon they are in bed and "For play, little they slept that night." There is a sting in the tail though. Fairies demand honesty of humans but fairy lovers almost always insist that they are asked no questions and that their relationship is concealed. Launval – like all such human lovers – breaches this vow of silence by boasting of his partner and "all that he had before won/ Melted away, like snow in the sun." He loses his lover and all her rich gifts.

There is nearly always a price to pay for loving a fairy. If it is not abandonment, the lover will instead sicken and die for longing, will be trapped in fairy land for ever or, after enjoying great pleasure with the maiden, will return home to find that not hours and days have passed as he imagined, but years and decades; all those he knew are married or dead and the world is changed irrevocably. These, then, are the fairy rules of love. Humans must be chaste and faithful, whereas fairies may be passionate, cruel, inconstant and selfish.

It will be observed that the code of conduct imposed upon humans is one of opposites and that the fairy nature is likewise a combination of polar contrasts.

For fortunate humans of the desired disposition, though, the fairies will be grateful and kind. Nonetheless, that which is most severely enjoined upon mortals is generally that behaviour which seems least important in fairy conduct. For instance, one should never steal from fairies, but their entire livelihood at times appeared to be predicated upon depredations from human society.

CHAPTER NINETEEN

They who must not be named

EUPHEMISMS AND FAIRY POWER

The open use of proper names for fairies – whether personal or collective names – is universally frowned upon and frequently punished. I want briefly to examine the nature of this rule and its motivations. Expert writer Katharine Briggs has described this superstition as the use of 'euphemistic' names for the fairy folk; I think that apotropaic may be a slightly more accurate term. The primary purpose of this allusiveness, I believe, is to turn away displeasure and ill-fortune.

Indirect names are used, I think, for several related purposes. The first is with a view to complimenting the fairy folk. Examples include the *Good People*, the *Good Neighbours*, the *Honest Folk*, the *Fair Family (Tylwyth Teg)*, the *Gentry*, the *People of Peace* and the *Seelie Court* – that is, the 'blessed court', which is matched by *Seelie Wicht*, a 'blessed soul'. Some names avoided impolitic directness but were simply descriptive, as with the Cornish *an pobel vean,* the little people. Sometimes the direct naming of things associated with the fairies was also avoided. Fridays were the favoured days of the *daoine coire* (the honest folk) in the Highlands and so a circumlocution replaced the word.[277]

The polite and honorary addresses often conceal a second motivation – and perhaps the most important – which is to avert the unfavourable attentions of the fairies. The invocations of goodness and peaceable conduct in part seek to ensure such a state of affairs: if you are respectful to them, they won't be so inclined to harm you. This is perhaps clearer in such names as *Bendith y mamau,* the mothers'

---

277 Campbell, *Superstitions of the Highlands and Islands of Scotland,* c.1.

blessing; a name surely aimed at deflecting the risk that the fairies will steal a human child and replace it with a changeling. The term is, in a sense, a spell to ward off the risk of abduction and the substitution of a sickly or demanding stock.

A final, very significant, element in this must be a desire to avoid using proper names directly. Across the globe in very many cultures it is known that a person's proper name has special powers and that it should never be used directly or without permission – for example, in Arabia the *jinns* are referred to as *mubarakin*, 'the blessed ones.' Names are a form of property with magical qualities; it was said that a fairy would be "baffled" if his proper name was discovered.[278] This explains many of the vaguely descriptive phrases employed – *the Green Coaties* or *Green Gowns, White Nymphs, People of the Hills, The Strangers* and *Themselves.*

This respectful avoidance of secret or personal names is best exemplified by the fairy tales featuring this theme. *Rumplestiltskin* is now the best known, thanks to the Brothers Grimm, but it is a German story, not a British one. Insular folklore has its direct parallels: the tales of *Tom Tit Tot, Whuppity Stourie, Terrytop* (Cornwall) and *Trwtyn Tratyn* from Wales. Possession of a being's concealed name gives control over that individual, hence the efforts to hide and to discover it. In one Welsh example, possession of the fairy maiden's name constrained her to marry a man.[279]

---

278 Wentz p.137.
279 Rhys p.45.

CHAPTER TWENTY

Pinch him, pinch him, blacke and blue

FAIRY BLIGHTS AND PUNISHMENTS

"Bring with thee airs from heaven or blasts from hell..."[280]

Our forebears had to have some way of explaining sudden illness and death, or the birth of a child which gradually was revealed to have mental disabilities. The cause ascribed for these afflictions, before the development of medical science, was the malign intervention of supernatural beings. It was the fairies that made people (and their livestock) ill; the benefit of this explanation was that it gave an understanding of an otherwise inexplicable malady and pointed to a solution – the propitiation of the 'good folk.'

It is possible to identify a range of means by which injury was believed to be inflicted:

- *pinching* – this was the primary fairy punishment for infringement of their codes and pinching is almost synonymous with faery: "like a fairy pinch that dainty skin."[281] They took reprisal for such infringements as:
  - *failing to keep a house clean and tidy* – the slovenly housewife or maid who failed to do her chores would be punished by the pixies pinching and taunting her; for example in *Nymphidia* Drayton notes of the house elves that "These make our Girles their sluttery rue/ By pinching them both blacke and

---

280 *Hamlet,* Act I, scene 4.
281 *England's Heroical Epistles,* 1597, Elenor Cobham to Duke Humphry.

blew." In Shakespeare's *Merry Wives of Windsor* the elves are commanded to "pinch the maids as blue as bilberry" wherever fires unraked or hearths unswept were found – because "Our radiant Queen hates sluts and sluttery."[282]

- *failing to put out clean water, milk and food* – if the fairies feel that a suitable welcome has not been prepared for them, they can be even more vindictive. Queen Mab, "with sharper nails remembers/ When they rake not up their embers."[283] Nips "from toe unto the head" were promised to maids who, by oversight, had not brought in clean water or spread the table and set out bread.[284]

- *spying upon fairy activities* – "Sawsie mortals must not view/ What the Queen of Stars is doing/ Nor pry into our Fairy woing" Endimion is warned in John Lyly's *Gallathea*. For his trespass, Endimion faces "sharp nailes to pinch him blue and red" and "spots ore all his flesh shall run."[285] In *The Merry Wives of Windsor* pinching is the fate to be meted out to Falstaff when he trespasses on the pretended fairy concourse;[286] and,

- *offences by lovers* – the fairies might punish lust and attempted rape or, conversely, the unkindness of lovers (see chapter 18). If any is found "forcing of a chastity" fairies are summoned to "pinch him to the bone/ Till his lustful thoughts be gone." In contrast, any lady "that did not kindly rue your paramours' harms" is warned that fairies "shall pinch black and blue/ Your white hands and fair arms;"[287]

- *jostling and bumping* – in a slightly more aggressive version of the former, a person who strayed into fairy precincts or who violated

---

282   Act IV scene 3.
283   Jonson, 'Entertainment at Althorpe,' 1603.
284   William Brown, *Britannia's Pastorals*, Book 1, song 2; see too *A description of the king of fairies clothes*, 1635, p.3.
285   *Gallathea*, 1584, Act IV, scene 3; in *The Mayde's Metamorphosis* Lyly also has those who come upon fairies dancing "pincht most cruelly."
286   Act V scene 5.
287   Fletcher, *The Faithful Shepherdess* III 1 and Thomas Campion, *Book of Ayres*, 1601.

their privacy might be pushed and misused in this manner, perhaps leading to at least partial paralysis. This was the fate of a farmer who invaded the fairy market on the Blackdown Hills and was left lamed on one side for the remainder of his life;[288]

- *blighting a farmstead* – if the fairies took against a person, plague might kill his cattle, weeds would infest his pastures and his harvests would wither;[289]

- *disrupting household tasks* – Dr Samuel Harsenet recorded the belief that if the proprieties of relations between humans and fairies were not observed they would take their revenge. If curds and cream were not left out at night "either the pottage was burnt next day in the pot, or the butter would not come, or the ale in the fat would never have good head."[290] The pamphlet *Robin Goodfellow, his mad pranks and merry jests* told a comparable tale. If no clean water was left out for the fairies' night time ablutions, "we wash our children in their pottage, milk or beer or whatever we find: for the sluts that have not such things fitting we wash their faces and hands with a gilded child's clout or else carry them to some river and duck them over head and ears."

- *punishments to match the fault* – if the fairy sense of propriety and decorum had been breached by a human, the sanction applied might be based upon the nature of the neglect. If a house was untidy, items would be concealed; if a house door had been left open by a maid servant, Robin Goodfellow would:

> "take them and lay them in the doore, naked or unnaked… there they lye, many time til broad day, ere they waken and many times against their wills, they show some parts about them that they would not have openly scene."[291]

If a person went to bed part dressed, their laces would be knotted so they could not be untied; if a face was left dirty, it would

288   Keightley, *Fairy Mythology*, pp.294-5.
289   Cromek, Appendix F.
290   *Declaration* pp.134-135.
291   *Robin Goodfellow, his mad pranks.*

be washed from the piss-pot; if horses were not combed, they would be daubed with soot and grease; if maids are lazy Puck would pull off the bedclothes and "lay them naked all to view" or would drag them onto the cold floor; if their heads were nitty or scabby the fairies would cut their hair "as close as an ape's tayle" or would slap on pitch so that the victim had to shave his or her own scalp.[292]

- *wasting sickness* – afflictions such as consumption might be ascribed to the sufferer being 'away with the fairies.' Instead of sleeping in his or her bed, at night the victim would in fact be dancing with the fairies. This ceaseless energetic activity sapped the strength and led to the person's decline and death. It was also believed that sadness at being parted from the fairies during the daytime contributed to the disease's progress and malignancy. John Aubrey recorded this belief as did the Reverend Robert Kirk when he described a woman whom he personally met who, after her encounter with the fairies, was "prettie melanchollyous and silent, hardly ever seen to laugh";[293]

- *physical assault* – a human might be shot with fairy arrows, resulting in total or partial paralysis and/ or death. These 'elf bolts' were the neolithic flint arrow heads turned up by cultivation, thereby giving context to otherwise mysterious artefacts. Robert Kirk remarked on the use of flint darts against livestock in the Highlands: the cattle would be injured internally without there being any outward sign of a wound, the blow by these elf bolts having "something of the Nature of Thunderbolt subtilty" . The resultant paralysis might be used to extract the "purest substance" of the beast for the fairies' consumption, or might help abduct an individual;

- *blinding* – a person whose eye(s) had been touched by fairy ointment, so that the spell of glamour was dispelled, might be blinded to ensure that they no longer saw the fairy folk. This could be done with a simple prod, or might be achieved with

---

292 *The pranks of Puck.*
293 *Secret Commonwealth of Elves and Fairies section 15.*

a breath, as in the poem *Sir Launfal*: the fairy maid Tryamour "blew on hir swych a breath/ That never eft might sche se;" and,

- *'fairy stroke'* – a fairy blast or a whirlwind might paralyse or prove to be fatal. The modern 'stroke' was formerly interpreted as the magical wounding of a person and was a recognised condition called 'the feyry.'[294] Rather than attacking with darts, a curse or spell inflicted epilepsy or paralysis and, once again, facilitated the abduction of the victim's soul. Kirk described how the fairies would smite "without Paine, as with a Puff of Wind."[295] The victim might be left lamed or similarly crippled for the rest of their life. This is the threatened fate of a man who was said to have angered Oberon by daring to "blab the secrets of the fayries."[296]

Finally, it should be noted that a number of other illnesses might also be blamed on fairies, including painful deformities, impetigo, childlessness and certain cattle pests. For example in the Highlands the spinal paralysis called *marcadh sidh* was believed to be engendered by fairies riding the livestock at night; indeed in Wales almost any livestock complaint was ascribed to the *Tylwyth Teg*.[297] It seems that in the late middle ages, a time of high infant mortality, 'feyry' was synonymous with childhood illness.[298]

In conclusion, in the absence of effective medical treatments, earlier generations had little to protect themselves from, or as remedies against, these conditions. What they did have available were the desperate measures of child abuse used against changelings, traditional herbal medicines and religion. The Reverend Kirk somewhat scathingly observed how congregations would swell periodically as local people attended church to "sene or hallow themselves, their Corns and Cattell, from the Shots and Stealth of these wandering Tribes." In confirmation of this statement, suspected witch John Walsh told his inquisitors in 1566 that fairies only had power over those who lacked religious faith.[299] The Reverend Kirk

---

294 Keith Thomas, *Religion & the Decline of Magic*, p.217.
295 S.4.
296 *The cozenages of the Wests*, 1613.
297 Wentz pp.86, 144 & 158.
298 Keith Thomas, *Religion and the Decline of Magic*, 1971, p.217.
299 see Thomas, *Religion and the Decline of Magic*, p.724.

also observed that the local country folk called the fairies *Sleagh Maith* (the Good People), in a further attempt "to prevent the Dint of their ill Attempts" and to deflect "these Arrows that fly in the Dark."[300] Resort might also be made to local 'cunning' folk for a cure. Just as fairies could cause illness, it was thought that they could grant healing powers to some. There are recorded witchcraft cases in which the accused ascribed their abilities to such supernatural aid (see chapter 33 later).[301]

Our transition to the modern, rational world has deprived us of many facets of our ancestors' lives – their intimate knowledge of animals and plants and their intense sense of community, for example – but those losses are balanced in some measure by an improved appreciation of the workings of nature and of history. Those flint arrow heads which so puzzled our forebears are now instantly assessed as 'Stone Age' by most people and placed easily within a geological timescale of millennia, divesting them of much of their mystery – if not their fascination. When a serving girl working for Alexander Carmichael felt a flint dart fly past her as she crossed the farmyard at night in the 1900s, her instinct was instantly to blame the nefarious *sidh* – even when naughty boys might have been a better explanation![302]

Lastly, the degree to which illness and death might be ascribed to fairies in considerable measure related to the popular assessment of fairy temperament. If they were seen as preternaturally ill-disposed towards humankind, almost anything might be blamed upon them.

---

300   Kirk section 2 and chapter 19 '*They who must not be named*'
301   see Thomas, *Religion and the Decline of Magic*, p.317.
302   see Wentz p.88.

Away with the Fairies

FAIRY ABDUCTIONS

Fairies were well known for their tendency to steal away humans, both adults and children.[303] Reginald Scot described how:

> "many such have been taken away by the said spirits for a fortnight or a month together, being carried with them in chariots through the air, over hills and dales, rocks and precipices, and pass over many countries and nations in the silence of the night, bereaved of their senses and commonly one of their members to boot."[304]

These experiences sound rather more like the flight of witches or the substance of many dreams. Fairy abduction might more typically occur in several ways:

- *by dancing in fairy rings* – this was a very common explanation of sudden disappearance. The victim might be lost for ever, might be danced to death or might return after a lapse of time. If the cause of the disappearance was deduced, the person could be rescued from the fairy ring on the anniversary of their disappearance, perhaps by force or by touching with iron;
- *by deception* – Cornish piskies lured away children, initially tricking them by appearing like a bundle of rags;[305]
- *by friendliness* – some humans are seduced away from their friends and family simply because the fairies are such pleasant

---

303 As a further illustration try the song *The Fairy Boy*, by Samuel Lover, 1840, performed by Lucy Ward on her 2011 album *Adelphi has to Fly*, Navigator Records.

304 *The Discoverie of Witchcraft*, book III, c.IV.

305 Hunt, *Popular Romances*.

company. Welsh girl Shui Rhys is one of these who preferred talking and playing with them so much that she never returned home;[306]

- *substitutes and changelings* – in chapter 16 I examined the notorious practice of the theft and replacement of babies (changelings): "by false fairies stolne away/ Whyles yet in infant cradle he did crall."[307] The same might from time to time happen to adults too. Folk lore displays a clear understanding of the fairies' practices. In a verse quoted earlier, Ben Jonson suggested that a ladle would replace an infant abductee. This suited his rhyme but is not a traditional concept. Sometimes, rather than a living being, a 'stock' was substituted – a log fashioned in the likeness of the missing person who was, in actuality, 'away with the fairies.' This motionless, speechless form (a "a lingering voracious Image" in the Reverend Kirk's words) was left at the home in bed to act as a cover for the fact that the man or woman had been taken to fairyland for some purpose – perhaps as a midwife or wet nurse to a fairy mother. In human society the person was believed to have died, but they lived on endlessly underground.[308] That was why persons long dead were often met by visitors to fairy land. Some readers will recall that in Susanna Clark's novel, *Jonathan Strange and Mr Norrell*, a bog-oak likeness is left in place of Lady Emma Pole who is abducted to dance at the fairy balls; and,

- *by kidnap* – as happened to the wife of Sir Orfeo in the poem of that name. Despite his precautions, surrounding her with one thousand well-armed knights, she was snatched from amongst them by the fairy king and no-one knew how. A much more modern version of the same practice comes from Scotland. John Roy of Abernethy recovered an Englishwoman carried off by the *sidh* by throwing them his hat and crying 'mine is yours and yours is mine.' The fairies have to comply with such a bargain.[309]

---

306 Sikes pp.67-69.
307 Spenser, *The Fairy Queen*, Book III, chapter 3, stanza 26.
308 Campbell, *Popular Tales of the West Highlands*, vol.2, 1890, p.65.
309 Keightley p.391; also p.297.

The passage of time in fairyland was different to that experienced on the earth. Abductees might find, for example, that:

- a few minutes with the fairies were in truth hours away from their friends – five minutes might turn out to be a year and a day and two hours two generations;
- a night was equivalent to one year, seven years, twenty years or many generations;
- a day in faery was in fact, on earth, a year and a day or even fifty years.

A long absence in fairyland brought many dangers to those returning:

- they might suffer the grief of finding parents deceased and former lovers married in their absence;
- they might perish as soon as human food passed their lips; or,
- they might crumble way to dust as soon as they touched a mortal.

These perils emphasise the risks of being 'away with the fairies' and how very different fairyland can be to the world of mortal men. Despite all of the foregoing, though, there is no consistency in the stories; there is no standard equivalent between earth time and fairy time and, for some, the time difference did not apply. Midwives could attend upon fairy mothers and return home the same evening; others who had friendly dealings with the fairy court could come and go at will, just as if they were visiting human friends in their homes.

CHAPTER TWENTY-TWO

A votaress of my order

OFFERINGS TO FAIRIES

One of the explanations of fairies is that they are the degraded remnants of former gods, the traces of ancient pantheistic belief in Britain. The habit of making offerings of one description or another to these beings lends support to this theory but, as we shall see, the evidence presents a confusing picture of what people understood themselves to be doing. The recorded practices could be worship, or they could even be something akin to a commercial transaction.

The offerings take several forms. The first is a general gift made to 'the fairies' as a sign of respect and propitiation. Several examples of this come from Scotland: in the Highlands and Islands it was common for milk to be poured on stones with hollows in them in order to ensure the protection of the herds of cattle. On top of Minchmuir, Peebles-shire, there was the so-called 'Cheese Well' into which locals threw pieces of cheese for the guardian fairies. If we see the fairies as once having been gods, then these marks of honour aimed at appeasing the 'good neighbours,' averting ill fortune and ensuring their continuing good will, appear to be strong confirmation of divine origins.

Similarly, on the isle of Lewis farmers would wade out into the waves and pour beer into the sea, invoking the water-spirit Shoney and asking for a good harvest of seaweed for the fields. Comparable conduct was found in the South West of England: miners would give up a portion of their lunches to the 'knockers' in the mine, hoping that they would then be led to the best lodes of tin, and at Newlyn the pixies living between low and high water mark, the *bucca,* would be offered a 'cast' of three fish so as to guarantee a good catch in the nets. These 'sacrifices' made with a view to a specific outcome are a very familiar aspect of human interactions with divinities. They also imply that the fairies possessed some kind of control over the sea and its contents. This is not a typical fairy attribute, although the Cornish spriggans were said to have power over the weather and could call on thunder and lightning when they wished to.

In England there is an example of a more direct exchange between human and fairy. There was a belief that elder trees were inhabited by the 'old lady of the elder tree.' If a person wished to cut some branches from a bush, a vow had to be made: 'Old Lady, if you let me take some of your wood now, you can take some of mine when I'm a tree.' Omission of this promise could lead to disaster – fire or illness in the household.

Secondly, there are examples of offerings being made in return for which a gift of money might be expected from the fairies. An example comes from Llanberis, in Snowdonia, from the 1750s: the practice was for farm maids to place a jug of fresh sweet milk and a clean towel on a stone in the morning. When they later returned, the jug would have been emptied by the *Tylwyth Teg* and a handful of coins would have been left. This kind of exchange between humans and fairies is very closely associated with the reports of fairies leaving small sums of silver for chosen people – albeit on the strict condition that they maintained secrecy as to the source of their new found prosperity. Violation of this would inevitably terminate the fairies' good favour. These practices clearly are a kind of bargain as much as an oblation. An interesting variant on this practice comes from North Wales:

> "a servant girl who attended to the cattle on the Trwyn farm, near Abergwyddon, used to take food to 'Master Pwca,' as she called the elf. A bowl of fresh milk and a slice of white bread were the component parts of the goblin's repast, and were placed on a certain spot where he got them. One night the girl, moved by the spirit of mischief, drank the milk and ate most of the bread, leaving for Master Pwca only water and crusts. Next morning she found that the fastidious fairy had left the food untouched. Not long after, as the girl was passing the lonely spot where she had hitherto left Pwca his food, she was seized under the arm pits by fleshly hands (which, however, she could not

see), and subjected to a castigation of a most mortifying character. Simultaneously there fell upon her ear in good set Welsh a warning not to repeat her offence on peril of still worse treatment." [310]

This might be read as either divine punishment for disrespect or simply revenge for a practical joke.

The exchanges just described were made in the open air or in uninhabited or deserted buildings. Throughout Britain, though, there was a very similar practice of householders leaving out bread, milk or clean, warm water for the fairies who visited their homes at night. Once again, a small gift might be anticipated in the morning. Sometimes, the coins were more like a reward – a clean and neat house was appreciated by the nocturnal visitors and was acknowledged by a couple of coppers. Some writers were in no doubt as to the underlying nature of these interactions. Robert Burton, in *Anatomy of Melancholy* (1621), understood fairies to be erstwhile deities

> "which have been in former times adored with much superstition, with sweeping their houses and setting of a pail of clean water, good victuals and the like, and then they should not be pinched but find money in their shoes and be fortunate in their enterprises."

Avoidance of punishment was a clear motivation: John Aubrey noted that, until the reign of King James I, country folk–

> "wont to please the fairies, that they might do no shrewd turnes, by sweeping clean the Hearth and setting by it a dish of fair water and halfe sadd bread, whereon was set a messe of milke sopt with white bread. And on the morrow they should find a groat." [311]

The last kind of fairy offering we should note is that made to known individual beings – most commonly the brownies and other domestic hobgoblins of English and lowland Scottish folklore. A kind of bargain is again involved in these cases. The brownie undertakes some "drudgery work" in the house or on the farmstead (threshing, mowing, cleaning)

---

310   Sikes p.22.
311   *Remains of Gentilisme & Judaism*, 1687 pp.29 & 125.

and gets remuneration. However, it was fundamental to the transaction that this gift of cream, milk or cake did not *seem* like a direct payment. The items were 'left out', available for the brownie to find and consume, but they were not explicitly given to the hobgoblin in return for the labours undertaken. If the offering was too plainly intended for the spirit – the worst examples being specially-made clothes to cover their hairy nakedness – then the brownie would take offence and would either leave the holding in a huff or, worse still, remain but as a malevolent presence (see too chapter 15).

An example of this tradition is found in Scot's *Discoverie of Witchcraft* (1584):

> "your grandams maides were woont to sett a boll of milke before … Robin Good Fellow for grinding of the malt or mustard and sweeping the house at midnight: and you have heard that he would chafe exceedingly if the maide or the goodwife of the house, having compassion on his nakedness, laid anie clothes for him, besides his messe of white bread and milke which was his standing fee."[312]

In his turn Milton, in *L'Allegro,* gives a similar account of the country dweller's stories of brownies:

> "Tells how the drudging goblin sweat,
> To earn his cream-bowl duly set,
> When in one night, ere glimpse of morn,
> His shadowy flail hath thresh'd the corn
> That ten day-labourers could not end;
> Then lies him down, the lubber fiend,
> And stretch'd out all the chimney's length,
> Basks at the fire his hairy strength;
> And crop-full out of doors he flings,
> Ere the first cock his matin rings."

---

312   Book IV, c.X.

A curious example of domestic interaction between humans and fairies which sits somewhere between the brownie and 'neatness rewarded' is a story from Stowmarket in Suffolk, recorded in the mid-nineteenth century. An old man in the town was regularly visited by the 'ferriers' or 'ferrishers' (as they were termed in the county) who used to meet in his home; he recalled that they wore long green coats and yellow shoes. He kept his house scrupulously clean for them and in return the ferriers supplied faggots which they put in his oven and, from time to time, would leave a shilling for him under a chair leg. When he spoke about these visits, he lost their favour. It's hard to say in this account who is more beholden to whom – there's an equality of exchange which obscures any suggestion of devotion.

The exact relationship between fairies and humans is, on the evidence of these examples, confused and ill-defined. This need not be too surprising, given that such uncertainty exists as to the origins of the fairy belief. In the first examples, maintaining the benevolence of the supernatural realm was a key element in the folk customs. The later examples, though, whilst made in propitiative guise, should really be seen as bargains. In return for labour or for food a payment is made; the pretence is that these are offerings but actual truth appears to be that the fairies are the supplicants, a relationship that Katherine Briggs identified when she spoke of the 'dependence of the fairies' upon humans.

CHAPTER TWENTY-THREE

From fairies ... guard me!

TALISMANS AGAINST FAERY FOLK

In the modern age, with the prevalent view of fairies as attractive and benign beings with whom we wish to make contact and commune, the concept of charms to protect ourselves from supernatural interference seems alien. However, as I have described previously, the view of faery was once very far from favourable and prophylactics were widely known.

The folklore evidence offers a variety of means of keeping oneself safe from fairy visitations. The recorded methods are:

- *iron and steel* – the supernatural race cannot abide forged metal in any form: the Reverend Kirk expressed it thus – "Iron hinders all the Opperations of those that travell in the Intrigues of these hidden Dominions."[313] In fact, metal is a double protection: the presence of iron items will prevent harm; touching with iron will drive fairies away. A scythe placed sharpened edge uppermost in a chimney will repel fairies; pins in the swaddling clothes, scissors hung over, or tongs laid upon, a cradle will prevent the substitution of a changeling (partly because the open blades will create a cross shape – see later); an iron bolt or lock on a door will guard a house, an axe placed under the pillow will protect the sleeper and striking a fairy with iron will result in its instant disappearance. In Wales the story of the fairy wife lost by accidentally striking her with the iron bit on a bridle was extremely common; contact with metal in these cases lost a loved one. Welsh folklore also records that if iron is thrown

---

313   Generally see Frazer, *The Golden Bough*, c.XXI, s.2 on the iron taboo; Kirk c.13.

at a changeling or at a clinging fairy, the unwelcome presence will instantly be repelled.[314] From time to time fairy hills will open and the sound of music will lure humans in; the best protective against never escaping is to place a knife at the exit so that the door cannot close again. If a person has been lured into dancing with the fairies in a ring, one way of recovering him or her is a touch with iron. Despite this widely attested aversion to ironmongery, it is curious to note that fairies will be found using metal items – in Wales they borrowed griddles and pots and there are regular stories of fairies asking humans to mend their implements. For example, a ploughman working in a field at Onehouse, just outside Stowmarket in Suffolk, was approached by a 'sandy-coloured' fairy for help mending his 'peel.' This was the long handled flat iron used for removing loaves from an oven. The ploughman easily repaired the broken handle and was very soon rewarded with hot cake fresh from the oven.

• *salt and fish* – an interesting tale from Cornwall tells of a cow that was favoured by the fairies for its milk. When the milkmaid at Bosfrancan farm near St Buryan realised what was happening, she sought advice from a local cunning woman who advised that the *pobel vean* could not abide the smell of fish or the savour of salt or grease. Her recommendation was to rub the cow's udders with fish brine to prevent the pisky thieving. The advice worked, but the cow thereafter pined for her supernatural friends.[315] Oddly, as mentioned in the previous chapter, fishermen in nearby Newlyn appeased the spriggans with an offering of fish, indicating that the revulsion was not consistent. In Wales it was said that one means of driving off a changeling was to place salt on a shovel, make the sign of a cross in it and then to heat it over the fire;[316]

• *turning clothes* – a consistently deployed protection was to 'turn your coat' – to turn a garment inside out as a way of defending oneself from fairy tricks. Two Cornish examples illustrate the

---

314 Rhys pp.23 & 250.
315 *Popular Romances of the West of England*, Robert Hunt.
316 Rhys p.103.

effectiveness of the remedy. A Mr Tresillian, returning late at night from Penzance to his home in St Levan, came upon the piskies dancing in their rings. He felt compelled to join them, at which point they swarmed upon him, stinging like bees. He retained enough presence of mind to turn his glove inside out and threw it at them, which instantly caused the throng to disappear. Secondly, an old widow living at Chy-an-wheal, above Carbis Bay, found that her home was favoured by the thievish spriggans of nearby Trencrom Hill. They resorted to her cottage to divide up their plunder and rewarded her tolerance of this by leaving her a coin after each visit. She hatched a plan to get more from them and, one night, secretly turned her shift inside out whilst the spriggans were present. This enabled her to seize a gold cup from them. The widow became a wealthy woman as a result, but she could never wear that shift again because, if she did, she suffered agonies.[317]

- *herbs* – certain plants are effective in repelling fairies. These include St John's Wort, red verbena, daisies, ash, four leaf clover (this plant has the virtue both of dispelling glamour and enabling a person to see fairy folk as well as repelling them), and rowan. For example, a branch of mountain ash will help pull a trapped person out of a fairy ring, as the fairies dread the tree.[318] Katherine Briggs suggests that it is the red berries of the plant which have given it its reputation for warding off evil, but it has much wider magical power than this, as Robert Graves explained in *The White Goddess*.[319] Lastly, there was a belief in Wales that a gorse hedge is excellent protection against unwelcome visitors.[320]

- *running water* – fairy folk are unable to cross streams and rivers, so in any pursuit leaping from bank to bank will be a sure escape for the hunted human. Water courses running south are said to be especially efficacious.[321] Oddly, nevertheless, fairies seem

---

317 *Popular Romances of the West of England*, Robert Hunt.
318 Rhys pp.85 & 246.
319 Graves, chapter 10.
320 Sikes, chapter IX, section II.
321 Campbell, *Popular Tales*, vol.2, p.69.

to have no objection to still water. They actively seek it out for washing themselves and they are from time to time associated with wells. For example there were several 'fairy wells' in Wales which demanded attention from local people, in the absence of which they would overflow or flood.[322]

- *faith* – according to suspected witch John Walsh, when he was examined in prison in 1576, fairies only have influence over those whose Christian faith is weak or absent. It may be questionable how much to rely upon this statement given the position he was in: he understandably wished to deflect the accusations made against him and, accordingly, he wanted to present himself as an orthodox individual who was resistant to any satanic temptations. Be that as it may, it was widely known that the sign of the cross would dispel supernatural threats. Wirt Sike gave an interesting summary of the Welsh beliefs in this respect: "There are special exorcisms and preventive measures to interfere with the fairies in their quest of infants. The most significant of these, throughout Cambria, is a general habit of piety. Any pious exclamation has value as an exorcism; but it will not serve as a preventive."[323]

- *ritual* – in south west Scotland it was believed that a fairy struck child could only be cured by laying it out on new, unbleached linen and washing it in water from a holy well, in silence, before sunrise and using a pitcher never before used. Its clothes had to be washed by a virgin but, after three such treatments, the child would thrive.[324]

- *self-bored stones* – according to John Aubrey, if a person could locate stones through which natural erosion had created a hole (sometimes called 'hag-stones'), they could protect their horses from night-riding by fairies by hanging the stones over each horse's manger in the stables – or by tying the stone to the stable key. The fairies would not then be able to pass underneath.

- *touching grass* – we have a record of a Welsh tradition that a

---

322 Rhys p.147 & chapter 6.
323 *British Goblins* p.63.
324 Cromek, Appendix F.

person may save themselves from fairy abduction by seizing hold of the sward, apparently because the *Tylwyth Teg* are prevented from severing blades of grass.[325]

- lastly, in the Scottish Highlands a variety of other substances were held to be efficacious against the fairies. These included fire and embers, which were carried around pregnant women and babies; oatmeal, which if carried in a pocket during a night time journey kept the traveller safe, and urine, sprinkled on cattle and about the house.[326]

---

325 Rhys pp.148 & 170.
326 Campbell, *Superstitions of the Highlands & Islands*, c.1.

CHAPTER TWENTY-FOUR

I conjure thee, Sybilia, o gentle virgin of fairies

HOW TO SEE FAIRIES

In the last chapter I considered ways of protecting oneself from supernatural attention. Some people, of course, have always actively wished to attract fairies to themselves and to be able to see them. Folk tradition recommends a number of ways of doing this:

- *being born with the gift* – some people have a natural ability to see fairies. In Wales this was felt to be fairly common – one in three people[327] – whereas the Reverend Kirk presented endowment with the second sight as a far rarer attribute. In *The Secret Commonwealth* he described the *'tabhaisver'* or seer as having more acute or 'exalted' vision than most. He explained that this was–

  > "a native Habit in some, descended from their Ancestors, and acquired as ane artificiall Improvement of their natural Sight in others; … for some have this Second Sight transmitted from Father to Sone thorow the whole Family, without their own Consent or others teaching, proceeding only from a Bounty of Providence it seems, or by Compact, or by a complexionall Quality of the first Acquirer."[328]

---

327 Wentz p.139.
328 Kirk c.12.

Even with this power though, the seer could only observe fairies provided they did not blink.

- *being rewarded with the gift by the fairies* – a Scottish man who unhesitatingly partook of fairy hospitality was granted the second sight for his good manners at the feast;[329]
- *being in touch with nature* – Tom Charman, resident of the New Forest, told Arthur Conan Doyle in the early 1920s that his gift of seeing fairies depended upon his being close to nature. He had seen them as a child but had then lost the gift for some time as he reached adulthood.
- *using a four leaf clover* – as described in chapter 10, a four leaf clover can protect against fairies but it can also reveal them, by dispelling their 'glamour.' For example, an old woman told how her nursemaid was able to see 'scores' of fairies swarming around her if she slipped a clover leaf into the grass pad used to carry a milk pail on her head;[330]
- *being in an odd numbered group of people* – a Monmouth schoolteacher reported that uneven numbers people were more likely to see fairies and that men were more likely than women;[331]
- *looking through an 'elf-bore'* – a piece of wood from which a knot has fallen out, leaving a hole through, is an ideal tool for seeing fairies. Hold the 'elf-bore' to your eye and, again, the glamour is dissipated. Kirk also recommended in chapter twelve of his book that the person look backwards through the fir knot;
- *certain light conditions* – as I have described in chapters 1 and 17, a person is more likely to see fairies at twilight, allegedly for physiological reasons. In the late nineteenth century on the Lleyn Peninsula it was believed that there was a greater chance of meeting the *Tylwyth Teg* on days when it was a little misty – when there was a light drizzle falling called *gwlithlaw* (dew-rain).[332] The cynical might remark that this means that most days will be

---

329 Cromek, Appendix F.
330 Wentz p.177.
331 Sikes p.106.
332 Rhys pp.36, 91 & 228.

good for seeing fairies in Wales…(!); what is not clear is whether these light conditions are favourable because they make faery more visible or because the Fair Folk prefer a little concealment;

- *physical contact* – being in contact either with the fairy or with a seer will transfer their magical sight. One might place a foot on that of the fairy – a Welsh farmer was accosted outside his home by a male fairy complaining that the human household's waste was draining down his chimney and into his house; when the farmer placed his foot on the other's, he was able to see below ground a house and a street of which he had never before been aware.[333] Alternatively one could have the power transferred by touching the seer in some special way: Kirk described how –

> "the usewall Method for a curious Person to get a transient Sight of this otherwise invisible Crew of Subterraneans, (if impotently and over rashly sought,) is to put his [left Foot under the Wizard's right] Foot, and the Seer's Hand is put on the Inquirer's Head, who is to look over the Wizard's right Shoulder, (which hes ane ill Appearance, as if by this Ceremony ane implicit Surrender were made of all betwixt the Wizard's Foot and his Hand, ere the Person can be admitted a privado to the Airt;) then will he see a Multitude of Wight's, like furious hardie Men, flocking to him hastily from all Quarters, as thick as Atoms in the Air";[334]

- *spells* – magic was the last certain means by which to be able to observe fairies. It could be used both to attract and then to 'bind' them – that is, to stop them disappearing again. In *The Discoverie of Witchcraft* Reginald Scot helpfully provides a selection of spells and procedures for these purposes.[335] Sibylia, the fairy queen, is commanded to appear quickly, and without deceit or tarrying, in a chalk circle before the summoner, "in the form and shape

---

333 Sikes p.71 & Rhys p.230.
334 c.12.
335 Book XV, chapter 8 & 9.

of a beautiful woman in bright and vesture white, adorned and garnished most fair..." If at first she does not appear, repeat the spell, 'for doubtless she will come.' I'll leave it up to readers to decide whether or not to give this a go...

CHAPTER TWENTY-FIVE

Rewards and Fairies

GIFTS FROM THE GOOD NEIGHBOURS

"It was told me that I should be rich by the fairies"[336]

In a previous chapter I discussed offerings to fairies and noted that the dividing line between worship and bargain was a difficult one to define with precision. I wish to return to this area, discussing here definite gifts from fairy-kind to humans. Welcome as this beneficence might be, it was undependable: Walter Scott warned that "although their gifts were sometimes valuable, they were usually wantonly given and unexpectedly resumed."[337] Furthermore, folklore writer Christine Emerick has pointed out the curious contrast between Celtic fairy gifts and those of the Teutonic elves. The former look valuable but prove to be worthless, whilst the latter are the reverse. In British folktales, there is a blending of these extremes.

This unprovoked benevolence could take a variety of forms:

- regular gifts of food or money might be found by a lucky individual – for instance, at Willie How barrow in Yorkshire a local man was told he would find a guinea coin on top of the burial mound every day, so long as he did not disclose his good fortune;
- a skill might be conferred upon a fortunate recipient, such as the ability to play the bagpipes;
- a helpful deed might be rewarded: in one Welsh story a farmer removed a rooks' nest from a tree near his crops. It had also

---

336 *Winter's Tale*, Act III, scene 3.
337 Sir Walter Scott, *Letters on Demonology*, letter IV.

overshadowed a fairy ring and they rewarded him for his act. Providing bathing water for fairy families would likewise receive more than its due;

- the provision of a service – such as carrying out a repair on a tool or acting as midwife – could be rewarded with more than the payment commensurate with the job. In another Welsh example, a midwife received a life time's supply of money for her assistance to the mother. A curious tale from Ipstones in Staffordshire describes a woman whose child was substituted for a changeling. Unlike most such maternal victims, she accepted the fairy child imposed upon her and cared for it as her own. In return, whenever she wished for money, it would appear. This bounty ceased when the infant sickened and died;

- as indicated by the last example, a gift or gifts might be given, or the lucky individual might more generally enjoy good luck and prosperity, with good fortune and bounty taking many forms in their lives. For instance, a highlander who gave his plaid to wrap a newborn fairy baby enjoyed good luck ever afterwards. A supply of inexhaustible food is variant upon this;

- there could be the gift of health and healing. Several sites are associated with this: passing a child through the *men an tol* in Cornwall could cure rickets; a well at Bugley in Wiltshire relieved sore eyes and the Hob Hole in North Yorkshire was beneficial against whooping cough in children. These properties might be conceived of as fairy beneficence or, perhaps, proof of their magic powers; and,

- lastly, there is the very old concept of the *fairy godmother* and her gifts to the new-born. This is recorded as early as the twelfth century in Layamon's *Brut*: when King Arthur was born "*alven hine ivengen; heo bigolen that child mid galdere swithe stronge*" – 'elves took him; they enchanted that child with magic most strong:' the fairies gave him riches, long life, prowess and virtues. These stories remained current in the seventeenth century, when Milton wrote how -

> "at thy birth, the fairy ladies daunc't upon the hearth,
> And sweetly singing round about thy bed
> Strew all their blessings on thy sleeping head."[338]

Fairy gifts were made to children as well as to adults. Indeed, anyone could attract the fairies' favour and there did not need necessarily to be a specific reason, although exercise of the fairies' esteemed virtues of generosity and hospitality tended to attract favourable attention: if a human is prepared to give freely they may enjoy the same in return. It did help, though, to accept the first gift readily and without conditions. Reginald Scot in *The Discovery of Witchcraft* recorded the tradition that fairies would favour servants and shepherds in country houses, "leaving bread, butter and chose sometimes with them, which if they refuse to eat, some mischief shall undoubtedly befall them by means of these fairies..."[339] Two stories confirm this belief. A man who mended a fairy's spade was rewarded with food. His companion counselled against eating it; the other cheerfully partook and benefitted for the rest of his life as a consequence of his spontaneous and trusting nature. Similar accounts come from Pensher, County Durham (plough horses die because the farmer refuses to eat the bread and butter left for him) and from Lupton in Westmorland, where the horse that ate the fairy food lived and the other which refused to do so perished.

Sometimes fairy generosity can become excessive, in that they will steal from others to benefit the preferred person. Neighbours' barns and granaries may be emptied in order to fill those of the blessed one.

> "[they] give me jewels here... oh, you must not tell though."[340]

However, fairy gifts are made subject to a strict rule that they are respected and are not disclosed. In all the cases so far mentioned, boasting about receiving gifts of money from the fairies would guarantee that the bounty would terminate. In one sad case, a boy who found regular small sums of money was beaten by his father on suspicion of being a thief. He finally confessed which instantly ended the family's good fortune, much

---

338   *Vacation Exercise.*
339   Book III, c.iv.
340   Ben Jonson, *The Silent Woman.*

to the parents' bitter regret.[341] Loss of the bounty could be the least of the penalties inflicted for want of discretion though: Massinger in *The Fatal Dowry* warns "But not a word of it – 'tis fairies treasure/ Which but revealed brings on the blabber's ruin"[342] whilst in *The Honest Man's Fortune* we are likewise reminded of this fact: "fairy favours/ Wholesome if kept, but poison if discovered."

Closely related to this condition are the *gwartheg y llyn*, the lake cattle, which are frequently brought to marriages by lake maidens or which mingle and interbreed with human herds. If the wife is later rejected or insulted, her departure will also inevitably mean the departure of the fairy beasts. The same is bound to occur if the human farmer tries to slaughter the fairy cattle, as this too will be interpreted as demonstrating a want of respect for the owners/ donors.

---

341 Rhys pp.37-38.
342 Act IV, scene 1.

Fairies and megaliths

There is a longstanding association between the fairies and barrows and megaliths, not just in Britain but across Europe; for example, in Cornwall spriggans are said *only* to be found near cairns, cromlechs, barrows and stones.[343] In earlier ages the fairy label was habitually chosen for these unexplained monuments. It may just have been a name – for instance, the Fairy Toot, in Somerset, Elf Howe near Folkton in Yorkshire, Fairy Knowe on Orkney, the *Pookeen* stone circle (the place of fairies/ pucks) at Clodagh, Co. Cork or the Fairy Stone (*La Grand Menhir Brisee*) in Brittany – but not infrequently fairies would be regarded as being more actively involved in the making of a site. The *Champs les Roches* stone rows in Brittany were made by fairies dumping stones they had been carrying; similarly, *Tregomar* menhir was dropped by a passing fairy. The *allee couverte* at Coat Menez Guen bears the marks of fairy fingers on two of its stones.

The extent of the fairy associations could vary:

- *music and dancing* – at Athgreany stone circle in Co. Wicklow the fairies play their pipes there at midnight; the fairies are also said to dance around the Hurle Stane in Northumberland. Numerous Dorset *tumuli* are remembered as 'music barrows' where, if you sit at midday, you will hear fairy music within – for example at Bottlebrush Down, near Wimbourne and also at Ashmore, Culliford Tree, Bincombe Bumps and Whitcombe;
- *healing* – the healing powers ascribed to the unusual holed stone arrangement at *Men an Tol*, Penwith, derive from the pisky linked to the site; and,

---

343 Hunt, *Popular Romance*; see too Roney-Douglas, *The Faery Faith*, pp.26-34.

- *dwellings: under stones* – most commonly, ancient stones are sites of supernatural habitation, in one way or another. Passage graves are dwellings themselves – for example in Brittany at Barnenez, *La roche aux fees* and at *La grotte aux fees*, which the supernatural inhabitants are supposed to have deliberately wrecked; a Cornish fogou near Constantine was called 'the pixie house' and in Ireland several stone circles are classified as *lios*, fairy forts, for example Grange in Limerick and Lissyviggeen in Kerry. The Irish legend is, in fact, that after their defeat by the invading Milesians, the fairy tribe of the *Tuatha De Danaan* retreated into an enchanted kingdom beneath raths and stones – such places as Newgrange, Dowth and Knowth in the Boyne valley now being their abodes. Ancient stones marking the access to fairyland are a common account throughout the British Isles – a hole or stairs beneath a *menhir* would lead to the faery realm. The Humberstone in Leicestershire is a fairy dwelling, as too is St John's Stone in Leicester itself. Lastly, John Aubrey tells of the large stone lying at Borough-hill near Frensham, Surrey. Locals could knock upon it and declare whatever they wished to borrow; a fairy voice would then tell them when to return and the item would be there;[344]
- *dwellings: under burial mounds* – various ancient burial mounds are recalled in folk memory as the fairies' homes: examples are to be found on Cley Hill in Wiltshire, at Cauldon Low and Long Low in Staffordshire (upon both of which the fairies were also known to dance, at the latter on Christmas Eve) and at Hob Hurst's House, Deepdale and Monsal Dale in Derbyshire. It may be noted in passing that some of the stones linked with the fairies are in fact the remaining internal elements of tumuli, the so-called cromlechs such as Pentre Ifan in Wales and (it has been suggested) *Men an Tol* in Penwith.

Given the supernatural link to stones and *tumuli*, it was inevitable that people would invest the sites with magical powers. We have seen the curative properties of *Men an Tol;* conversely in Ireland and Scotland

---

344   Aubrey, *Natural History of Surrey,* vol.3, p.366.

interference with or damage to stones was avoided through fear of fairy revenge. In Ireland the belief persists that disturbance could lead either to crops or the home burning; in the Highlands Rev. Kirk recorded a prohibition upon taking turf or wood from a *sithbruaich* (a fairy hill); similarly, tethering an animal by pinning it down on the knoll was very unpopular with the fairy inhabitants within.[345]

Standing stones themselves have also been invested with spiritual power. Whether this is ascribed to their siting upon ley lines, or to fairy residents, it is still an element of our beliefs about standing stones.

---

345 Campbell, *Superstitions of the Highlands and Islands of Scotland*, c.1.

PART TWO

British Fairies in
Art and Literature

"He is as English as this gate, these flowers, this mire,
And when at eight years old Lob-lie-by-the-fire,
Came into my books, this was the man I saw,
He has been in England, as long as dove and daw."

From *Lob* by Edward Thomas.

CHAPTER TWENTY-SEVEN

Nymphes and faeries

RENAISSANCE INFLUENCES UPON THE 'NATIONAL FAIRY'

The fairy as conceived by British folk tradition was affected – and not for the better – by the revival of classical learning in the sixteenth and seventeenth centuries. In this chapter I wish to trace the course and impact of this rebirth of Roman and Greek knowledge in the specific context of British fairy lore.

The very earliest sign of classical influence comes from Chaucer, in the *Merchants Tale*. He refers there to -

> "Pluto, that is the king of fayerye
> And many a lady in his companye
> Folwinge his wyf, the quene Prosperpyne."

This verse can be dated to about 1390 and is probably more a sign of Chaucer's own education and reading than any real indicator of the spread of new thinking from Italy, where the *rinascimento* was at that time still in its infancy. Equally, though, John Gower in his *Confessio Amantis* of 1386 tells the tale of Narcissus, and mentions "such a Nimphe, as tho was faie."[1]

I suggest that a more significant start date for the popular use of classical allusions is the appearance of Gavin Douglas' 1513 translation of Ovid's *Aeneid*, in which he chose to refer to "nymphis and faunis apoun every side/ Quhilk Fairfolkis or than Elfis clepen we..." This linking of nymphs and elves remains consistent then for the next 150 years; for example, Thomas Nash makes this analogy: "The Robin Goodfellows,

---

1   *Confessio Amantis*, 1386-90, Book 1.

Elfs, Fairies, Hobgoblins of our latter age, which idolatrous former days and the fantastical world of Greece ycleped Fauns, Satyrs, Dryads and Hamadryads..." Latterly, Milton in *Comus* from 1630 spoke of fairies and elves as equivalent to nymphs. Of this work, Floris Delattre observed that, "the now trite assimilation of English fairies to classical nymphs gains ... a fresh beauty" thanks to the poet's "refined language."[2]

Translations of Ovid soon spread other classical concepts: for example Thomas Phaer in his 1550 version of the *Aeneid* mentioned fauns, nymphs and the fairy queen whilst Arthur Golding's translation of the *Metamorphoses* of 1565 described "nymphes of faery." The process could work in reverse as well, with native terms being used to explain classical ones. For example, Golding felt that the best translations he could make were to describe the "Chimaera, that same pouke" and to render 'naiads' as "water-fairies."

The easy reference to classical deities then became habitual. Nymphs and fairies were inseparable: poet William Browne learned about the 'dancing fairies' from a 'wood-nymph;' Drayton in *Poly-Olbion* treats "Ceres nymphs" as interchangeable with fairies and also marries a nymph to a fay and has dryads, hamadryads, satyrs and fauns dance with fairies in his *Nymphals* 8 and 6.[3] Other Greek and Roman figures also begin to insinuate themselves. Scot in *The Discovery of Witchcraft* (1584) mentions "satyrs, pans, fauns, sylvans, tritons, centaurs..." in his list of fairy beings and he names the fairy queen variously as Sibylla, Minerva, Diana and Herodias.[4] For King James VI in *Daemonologie* Diana and her court are synonymous with 'Phairie.' Ben Jonson's *Masque of Oberon* from 1610 carelessly mixes the "coarse and country fairy" with satyrs and sylvans. Burton, writing the *Anatomy of Melancholy* in 1621, listed such "Terrestrial devils [as] *lares, genii,* fauns, satyrs, wood nymphs, foliots, fairies..." Spenser meanwhile introduced the Graces to the company of fairies in both *The Fairy Queen* and *Epithalamium.*

It may be helpful to provide a summary of the various Greek and Roman gods and spirits with whom parallels were so freely drawn. It must

2   *English Fairy Poetry,* 1908, p.165.
3   Browne, *Britannia's Pastorals,* Book 2, song 4; Drayton, Song XXI.
4   Book VII c.XV.

be acknowledged that there are undeniable parallels and comparisons between some British fairies and some Mediterranean deities, analogies sufficiently strong to justify a few of the identifications made. This is, of course, due to the fact that all of these supernatural beings derive ultimately from the same Indo-European sources and are responses to the same natural processes and features. Nonetheless, each culture had developed differently and whilst there were links to be made (as, for example, was done in works such as Frazer's *Golden Bough)* these beings had evolved separately for centuries and, whilst comparable, were very far from being identical.

Writers freely made reference to:

- *Abundantia* – who was the Roman goddess of fortune and prosperity. She evolved into a beneficent spirit and, ultimately, into Habundia, queen of the witches and fairies;
- *Ceres* – she was a goddess of the growth of plant foods. Insofar as she had vegetative associations, there was some tenuous link with British fairies;
- *Diana* – who was the virgin goddess of childbirth, of nature and of the moon. Queen Mab was a midwife, as testified by Andro Man, accused of witchcraft in 1598, and fairies often danced in the moonlight, so that Diana's transfer to Britain makes some sense;
- *Dryads* – nymphs of trees and woods and so comparable to elves;
- *Fauns* – a faun is a rural deity who bestows fruitfulness on fields and cattle. He can also have prophetic powers. His influence over natural processes suggested the analogy with elves;
- *Genii* – are clan spirits and perhaps therefore allied to brownies, banshees and the like;
- *Graces* – these were Greek goddesses of fertility in fields and gardens and accordingly comparable to elves and fairies;
- *Hecate* – was the goddess of magic and spells; she was linked to the moon and was a goddess of childbirth and the night. Through Queen Mab she was therefore associated with fairies and witches;
- *Herodias* – was mother of Salome and was reputed to be head

of a witch cult. She became linked to fairies through the witch craze and was identified with *Habundia*, queen of Elfame. By circuitous routes, therefore, Heywood ended up equating sibils and fees, white nymphs, Nightladies and Habundia their queen;

- *Lares* – are tutelary deities of fields and homes and are accordingly similar to boggarts, brownies and such like. The equation between the classical model and the domestic spirit was readily made: we hear for example of "A round of fairie – elves, and larrs of other kind," or find Robin Goodfellow described as "a breecheless larr" or as "one of those *Familiares Lares*";[5]

- *Minerva* – was linked to the arts and crafts and had no real identity with British fairies;

- *Muses* – a character in William Browne's *Britannia's pastorals* disclaims any supernatural lineage, denying that she is "of the Fairie troop nor Muses nine,/ Nor am I [daughter of] Venus, nor of Proserpine..."[6] The muses are daughters of Zeus and goddesses of song, although they also have some links to streams and springs;

- *Nymphs* – these are minor deities linked to fertility, growth, trees and water (streams, lakes and the seas). As such they are clearly comparable to elves and fairies. For example, the nymphs tended to protect specific locales so that there may be some analogy to be made between the water naiads and British sprites like Grindylow and Peg Powler;

- *Pan* – was a deity of Arcadia, part-goat, part-human. He haunted the high hills and brought fertility to the flocks and herds, but not to agriculture. He could send visions and dreams. He has a vague resemblance to pucks and hobgoblins, but no more;

- *Satyrs* – were envisaged as half-man and half-beast; they were brothers to the mountain nymphs and akin to fauns. As such, they resembled pucks, brownies and hobgoblins to some extent;

- *Sibylla* – was a prophetess, and so became linked to fairies through the witch craze;

---

5   *The Shepherd's Dream* 1612 and *Tarlton's Newes out of Purgatorie,* 1590.
6   Book 1, song 4.

- *Sylvans* – these are woodland deities, readily associated with fairies.

Some of the classical names used had no relevance at all to British fairies; some denoted distantly related beings. All were facile and ultimately uninformative and unhelpful. The use of the classical comparisons diluted and disrupted more accurate knowledge of genuine British traditions, inhibiting rather than encouraging study. They were superficial displays of learning which detracted from a deeper and more valuable investigation of the 'national fairies' as Floris Delattre termed them. Classical references added nothing of value to the verse – rather it obscured the nature of insular tradition and accelerated its decline by promoting false analogies and parallels. Keightley was even harsher in his assessment: had the pastoral poets used the British fairy mythology exclusively and given up "all the rural rout of antiquity," he believed that "the pastoral poetry of that age would have been as unrivalled as its drama. But a blind admiration of classic models and a fondness for allegory were the besetting sins of the poets."[7] The Greek and Roman figures had character traits and qualities unknown before, with notions of hierarchy, worship and relationships that were alien and inapplicable to British folklore. All in all, therefore, the impact of the Renaissance learning was in this instance entirely negative.

To conclude, we must first concede that British fairy lore was already a hybrid, containing elements of Celtic, Saxon and French myth; Morgan le Fay mixed with Germanic elves and Cornish pixies to create complex and many layered stories. Classical themes added nothing to this. References to nymphs and fauns were a learned and literary graft upon native roots and served only to stunt further development of the tradition. Whatever the wider enriching qualities of the Renaissance, it only did damage to British folk lore. A final example of the depth of confusion plumbed by the early seventeenth century is apparent from Fletcher's *Faithful Shepherdess,* in which a character declares that:

---

7   *Fairy Mythology,* p.342.

"No goblin, wood-god, fairy, elf or fiend,
Satyr or other power that haunts these groves,
Shall hurt my body..."[8]

Classical learning has been compounded by the Protestant hysteria about witches to completely obscure the identity of the traditional British fae.

---

8   Act I, scene 1.

CHAPTER TWENTY-EIGHT

Fear of little men

OR HOW THE FAIRY GOT HER WINGS

In William Allingham's poem *The Fairies* (1883) he gives late expression to a formerly common attitude to fairies:

"Up the airy mountain,
Down the rushy glen,
We daren't go a-hunting
For fear of little men;
Wee folk, good folk,
Trooping all together;"

The traditional terror of fairies and the change in attitudes in more recent times is something I have touched upon in an earlier chapter and which I wish to analyse in more detail here.

Until at least the early seventeenth century, the conventional view of fairy kind was that they were as dangerous as they were intriguing and enticing. For example, the eller maids of Denmark were beautiful, but also deadly: anyone lured into dancing with them would be danced to death; they would never be able to stop and would perish from exhaustion. Fairies were the causes of disease and stole human children, food and possessions.

What I wish to examine here is how these fearsome and sometimes fatal creatures could deteriorate into something cloyingly cute and eminently suitable for little girls to imitate. In *Religion and the Decline of Magic* Keith Thomas prefaced his discussion of fairy beliefs by observing that "Today's children are brought up to think of fairies as diminutive beings of a benevolent disposition, but the fairies of the Middle Ages were neither small nor particularly kindly."[9] When was our fearful respect for the fairies replaced by a simpering, indulgent affection?

I have dated the change, as I suggest, to around 1600. Shakespeare provides us with some evidence of the shift in popular perceptions. Some commentators view him as the sole culprit, but this is to imbue him with far greater influence and respect than he had at the time. He may now be seen as a genius and cultural icon, but that was not his status in his lifetime; as a playwright he did not shape views, but he certainly does reflect them.

Take, for example, *Midsummer Night's Dream*. On the one hand there is Puck, whose magic interventions in human affairs might be dismissed as farcically inept, but who should probably best be viewed as mischievous, if not malignant, in his conduct. He admits to revelling in his tricks, for certain. At another extreme are the fairies introduced by Titania to Bottom, called Peaseblossom, Cobweb, Moth and Mustardseed; here we have a first hint of the tiny and harmless beings with whom we are so familiar today. A sense of these fairies' size is conveyed by their use of glow-worms as lanterns and their hiding in acorn cups to escape Oberon's fury. By contrast, there is the encounter in *The Merry Wives of Windsor* between Sir John Falstaff and some children disguised as fairies. They may be small, but that does not in the least detract from the horror he feels: "They are fairies; he that speaks to them shall die: I'll wink and couch: no man their works must eye."[10] Lack of stature, for Shakespeare's contemporaries, still did not of necessity denote weakness or an amenable nature.

Nevertheless, other writers picked up upon Shakespeare's use of tiny, charming fairies and developed the theme very strongly in the literature of the early seventeenth century. Tom Thumb is listed amongst the fairies and goblins by Reginald Scot and, in one text of 1630, he is described as being "but an inch in height, or a quarter of a span." He suffers such misfortunes as being carried off by a raven because of his size. Lyly in the *Maides Metamorphosis* has the 'First fay' state "Then I get upon a fly,/ Shee carries me above the sky." Jonson's *Sad Shepherd* of 1641 mentions "span long elves" (that is, nine inches or 23 centimetres) and the 1633 play

9   1971, p.724.
10   Act V, scene 5.

Fuimus Troes by Jasper Fisher alludes to "Fairies small, two feet tall."[11] Once established, writers began to elaborate upon and have fun with these concepts. Drayton has fairies hiding in hazelnut shells and sailing in an acorn cup, *Britannia's Pastorals* has bread made of hazel kernels and a dish of three fleas in a sauce. Herrick pursues the same ideas to an extreme degree in his descriptions of Oberon and Queen Mab. By the time of Alexander Pope, the fairy king and queen had been reduced to weightless pygmies.[12]

With the shrinking came a loss of awe. A tone of disrespect began to appear in mentions of elves, so that we encounter references to 'mawmets',[13] puppets,[14] apes [15] and urchins.[16] Fairies are reduced to something doll-like and harmless and are no longer threatening. This attitude of cynical and dismissive rationalism reaches an apogee in a speech by Mopsus in the play *Amyntas*. He rejects the idea of a fairy bride and refuses to "wooe a gnat ... I must have flesh and blood ... A fig for fairies!"[17]

Whilst poets and playwrights delighted in exploiting the literary potential of microscopic fairies, what other changes were taking place? I think that there is a number of causes for the loss of fairy faith. The growth of science and industry, particularly in the eighteenth and nineteenth centuries, removed the justification for and threat of fairies. Previously, as Geoffrey Parrinder remarked, "they helped explain many of the curious happenings of life."[18] By the later 1600s, this function was being superseded as John Aubrey wrote:

"*Old wives tales* – Before printing old wives' tales were ingenious, and since Printing came into fashion, til a little before the Civil-Warres, the ordinary Sort of People were not taught to read; nowadayes bookes are common, and most of the poor people understand letters; and the many good bookes, and a variety of Turnes of affaires; have

---

11   Act I, scene 5.
12   *January & May,* 1709.
13   *The Maydes Metamorphosis,* act II, scene 2.
14   *The Tempest,* act V, scene 1; *Amyntas,* act II, scene 6 & Robert Herrick, *The Fairie Temple.*
15   Drayton, *Nymphidia.*
16   *The Maydes Metamorphosis,* act II, scene 2 & Rowlands, *More Knaves Yet?*
17   Act II, scene 6.
18   *Witchcraft,* Pelican, 1958, p.70.

putt all the old Fables out of doors and the divine art of Printing and Gunpowder have frightened away Robin Goodfellow and the Fayries."[19]

When they were no longer required to explain illness, they were left as merely decorative and un-threatening. That said, if fairies had become redundant in this environment, their social function could be preserved by transporting them to other worlds. This appears to be what has happened: green clad goblins have been translated into the 'little green men' of science fiction.

Secondly, rationalism and religious scepticism has had a role. Disbelief in a spirit world is sufficient to kill off fairies entirely, but it has also stopped them being taken seriously. Once this had happened, their descent into cuteness and whimsy was easy.

Fairy belief for a long time was treated as a thing of the previous generation. For instance, John Aubrey recalled that "when I was a Boy, our Countrey people would talke much of them..." meaning 'Faieries'. His contemporary, Sir William Temple, said much the same thing, suggesting that fairy belief had only really declined over the previous thirty years or so (i.e. during the mid-seventeenth century). Robert Burton, writing the *Anatomy of Melancholy* in 1621, shared these opinions: fairies had been "in former times adored with much superstition" but were now seen only from time to time by old women and children.

Nevertheless, doubt seems to have been well established by the 1580s at least. The best evidence for this is Reginald Scot's *The Discoverie of Witchcraft* of 1584. The book is an assault upon belief in witches, but he compares this extensively with the parallel belief in a supernatural race of beings. In his introduction 'To the reader' Scot remarks that:

"I should no more prevail herein [i.e., in persuading his audience] than if a hundred years since I should have entreated your predecessors to believe that Robin Goodfellow, that great and ancient bull-beggar, had been a cozening merchant and no devil indeed. But Robin Goodfellow ceaseth now to be much feared..."

---

19   *Remains of Gentilisme & Judaisme*, 1687-89, p.68.

Once again, the fairy faith is a thing of the (distant) past. Later Scot comments that "By this time all Kentishmen know (a few fooles excepted) that Robin Goodfellow is a knave."[20] Scot's theme is that such credulity is not just old-fashioned; it is now the preserve of the simple and weak. He repeats these allegations throughout his text:

> "the feare of manie foolish folke, the opinion of some that are wise, the want of Robin Goodfellow and the fairies, which were woont to mainteine chat and the common people's talke in this behalfe … All which toies take such hold upon men's fansies, as whereby they are lead and entised away from the consideration of true respects, to the condemnation of that which they know not."[21]

Likewise we are informed later that:

> "we are so fond, mistrustful and credulous that we feare more the fables of Robin Goodfellow, astrologers and witches and beleeve more things that are not than things that are. And the more unpossible a thing is, the more we stand in feare thereof."[22]

Talk of fairies then, was in Scot's opinion only fit for "yoong children" and its only purpose was to "deceive and seduce." Scot is concerned how many in the past were "cousened and abused" by such tales and he admonishes his readers to remember this:

> "But you shall understand that these bugs speciallie are spied and feared of sicke folke, children, women and cowards, which through weakness of mind and body are shaken with vain dreams and continuall feare… But in our childhood our mothers maids have so terrified us with … urchins, elves, hags, fairies… that we are afraid of our own shadowes."[23]

Scot remained confident in the advance of reason, however:

---

20   Book XVI, c.7.
21   *The Epistle.*
22   Book XI, c.22.
23   Book VII, c.15.

"And know you this, by the waie, that heretofore Robin Goodfellow and Hobgoblin were as terrible and also as credible to the people as hags and witches be now, and in time to come a witch will be as derided and contemned, and as plainlie perceived, as the illusion and knaverie of Robin Goodfellow."[24]

King James I/VI in his *Daemonologie* (1597) was just as scornful as Scot of any belief in 'Phairie' but he did not ascribe it to mere foolishness. For him, it was more sinister – it was a deception of the devil who had "illuded the senses of sundry simple creatures, in making them beleeve that they saw and harde such thinges as were nothing so indeed." Although the fairy faith was "one of the illusiones that was risest in the time of Papistrie" it was thankfully in decline in Presbyterian Scotland at the time that he wrote.[25] By 1734, and the publication of the pamphlet *Round About our Coal Fire,* fairies had dwindled to the subject matter of fond childhood recollections. The author laughs and shakes his head at what he was persuaded to believe in his infancy by nursemaids. He knows now that the bangs and crashes at night were merely the servants romping in the kitchen whilst the stories of hobgoblins and 'buggy-bows' were just used to scare small children to bed and out of the way of the grown-ups.[26]

Thirdly, fairy belief dwindled as the natural world was increasingly explored, surveyed and quantified. When every acre of land was being assessed for its productive value and as a capital asset, the fairies were mapped and measured out of existence. On a crowded island, no space was left for anything except the tiniest of beings to survive. In fact, even as early as the first quarter of the seventeenth century, Michael Drayton could equate smallness with fairy nature: in his *Eighth Nymphal* he declared "Why, by her smallness you may find/ That she is of the fairy kind."

The cumulative effect of these societal changes was, as Keith Thomas wrote, that "By the Elizabethan age, fairy lore was primarily a store of mythology rather than a corpus of living beliefs."[27] Deprived of its

24   Book VII, c.2.
25   c.V.
26   Chapters II & VI.
27   *Religion and the Decline of Magic,* 1971, p.726.

rationale, the decay set in quickly. There is a suggestion of flight (as well as of insubstantiality) in Drayton's *Poly-Olbion* – "The frisking fairy there, as on the light air borne"[28] but explicit winged flight is first mentioned in *The Rape of the Lock* from 1712, in which Alexander Pope imagined fairies "Some to the sun their insect wings unfold/ Waft on the breeze or sink in clouds of gold." When, in 1798, Thomas Stothard illustrated Pope's book with fairies with butterfly wings, the trend was confirmed. Contemporaneously, we may note a bat winged Puck by Fuseli from 1790 and a tiny winged fairy creature in his illustration of Titania awakening with Bottom dated to 1794. Writing his *Song of the Pixies* in 1793, Samuel Taylor Coleridge described how they would retreat to a shady hollow before the rising sun, lest "our filmy pinion/ We scorch amid the blaze of day." This manner of representation quickly seems to have become the convention: in subsequent Victorian images fairies are predominantly winged creatures; these wings are either gauzy like dragonflies' or patterned like butterflies'.

The poet John Clare, born in 1793, was brought up in the East Midlands countryside, but he was well acquainted with the literary conventions of tiny, delicate fairies and he faithfully reproduced these in his verse. His poem *Fairy Things* is a catalogue of diminutive natural wonders, such as lichen and fungi. A crocus half-opened is like "a sunbeam left by a fairy", a moth perched on a grass stem is "like a fairy" and the stamens of May blossom are "fairy pins amid the flowers."[29] Fairyland had by the early nineteenth century become synonymous with the cute and twee – at least for one who had done a little reading.

All the same, in some places and amongst some groups folk belief could still lag well behind popular culture and artistic representations: Ivor Gurney wrote a poem in 1918 that must preserve older Gloucestershire beliefs. Having waited in a lane at dusk for a lover to return home, he is alarmed by a bustle in the hedgerow:

---

28   1613, Song XXI.
29   *Recollections of an Evening Walk* and *The Flitting.*

"Until within the ferny brake
Stirred patter-feet and silver talk
That set all horror wide awake-
I fear the fairy folk."[30]

In 1890 J. G. Campbell recorded fairy beliefs in the Western Highlands. The stories were still 'firmly believed' and people hesitated to discuss their good neighbours because "they are amongst them and about them."[31] There have been stubborn resisters too to the sentimentalising tendency. Rudyard Kipling in *Puck of Pook's Hill* made clear his feelings; Puck tells Dan and Una:[32]

"Besides, what you call [fairies] are made up things the People of the Hills have never heard of – little buzzflies with butterfly wings and gauze petticoats, and shiny stars in their hair, and a wand like a school-teacher's cane for punishing bad boys and rewarding good ones... Can you wonder that the People of the Hills don't care to be confused with that painty-winged, wand-waving, sugar-and-shake-your-head set of impostors? Butterfly wings indeed!"

The ultimate result of this decline is some of the twee horrors to be found. For Christmas, I received a card bearing an illustration by Ida Rentoul Outhwaite. Along with Cicely Mary Barker, she is one of the prime offenders in the genre loathed by Kipling (and Puck). Amongst her pictures you will find fairies with perfect 1920s bobs and, worse still, gambling with koala bears at drinks parties... The resistance to the sentimentalising tendency continues, but after at least a century, it may sadly be a losing battle.[33]

---

30 *Girl's Song*, September 1918.
31 *Popular Tales of the West Highlands*, 1890, vol.2, p.81.
32 1908, p.14
33 see for example the remarks of Cassandra Lobiesk on her website *Fae Folk: the world of fae.*

CHAPTER TWENTY-NINE

Full of Fairy elves

WILLIAM BLAKE AND FAIRIES

The poet William Blake had a very clear vision of the nature of fairies, although these thoughts were frequently unique to him – not an uncommon situation in the complex mythology that he elaborated over the course of his life! Blake spoke of "the elemental beings called by us by the general name of fairies." From this it seems clear that he did not conceive of a single class of supernatural being, but of complex variety – as is, of course, the British conception of fairy-kind.

In his verse, Blake's fairies fulfil a number of functions:

- primarily and originally they are remnants of the pagan gods of Britain. In *The Four Zoas* Blake speaks of the "fairies of Albion, afterwards The Gods of the Heathen."
- they are emanations of his character *Los* (broadly 'time and space') and accordingly they are the makers of time. In *Milton* time is described as "the work of fairy hands of the four elements."[34]
- along with nymphs, gnomes and genii, fairies are spirits that animate the material, vegetative world – they are the "rulers of the vegetable world."[35] They are often associated by Blake with flowers and natural growth and they are linked to natural vigour and fecundity. For example in 1802, after his move to Felpham on the Sussex coast, Blake wrote that the trees and fields roundabout his cottage were "full of Fairy elves." The fairy that dictates *Europe* to the poet is first discovered "sat on a streak'd Tulip." The fairies

---

34   28, 60.
35   Preface to the 'Descriptive Catalogue.'

represent the element of air, whilst nymphs are water, genii fire and gnomes earth. These elements can be positive and beneficial, but they have a darker side too. They can become "ravening deathlike Forms,"[36] in which aspect they are–

> "unforgiving and unalterable …
> … they know only of Generation:
> These are the Gods of the Kingdom of the Earth, in contrarious
> And cruel opposition, Element against Element, opposed in War…"[37]

In this form the fairies join the giants and the witches and ghosts of Albion in the dance of death with Thor and Freya and "lead the moon along the Valley of Cherubim."[38]

- fairies are a little like witches' familiars and each person appears to have their own, personal fairy, a sort of guardian angel perhaps.[39] In one fragment of verse Blake describes Joseph of Arimathea speaking to "My fairy."
- the fairies love music and dance in fairy rings, in line with established tradition [40]
- they act as spiritual protectors: Blake's visionary city of Golgonooza has four gates – 64,000 genii guard the eastern gate, 64,000 gnomes the northern, 64,000 nymphs the western and the southern gate is guarded by 64,000 fairies.[41]
- closely related to the previous characteristic, fairies are understood to be intimately aware of the sensuous nature of life. In *Europe*, for example, the fairy offers to open Blake's senses and to "shew you all alive/ The world, where every particle breathes forth its joy." He demonstrates that the material world is not dead; rather

---

36   *Jerusalem* 36.
37   *Milton* 34.
38   *Jerusalem* 63.
39   See for example the poems *William Bond* and *Long John Brown and Little Mary Bell*.
40   See *A Fairy Leapt Upon my Knee*.
41   *Jersusalem* I, 13; indeed, the entire poem is offered by Blake because his former giants and fairies had met with a favourable reception.

each flower whimpers when it is plucked and its eternal essence then hovers around Blake "like a cloud of incense." In this respect, then, fairies represent the natural state of human imagination and perception, before it has been blunted and enslaved by logic and reason. In his *Motto to the Songs of Innocence and Experience*, Blake condemns how:

> "The good are attracted by men's perceptions,
> And think not for themselves;
> Til experience teaches them to catch
> And to cage fairies and elves."

- the keen animation of the fairy senses seems to shade into sensuality and Blake makes some connection between these spirits and female sexuality. In 'A fairy leapt upon my knee' the spirit protests to Blake thus:

> "Knowest thou not, O Fairies' lord,
> How much to us contemn'd, abhorred,
> Whatever hides the female form
> That cannot bear the mortal storm?
> Therefore in pity still we give
> Our lives to make the female live;
> And what would turn into disease
> We turn to what will joy and please!"

Another verse treats the supernatural creature as 'king' of the marriage ring. It appears that Blake saw the emotional and physical obsession of love as some sort of spell that has to be broken. This link to carnal pleasure also seems to feature in his poem *The Phoenix*, sent to Mrs Butts in 1800 after the move to Felpham. Blake contrasts a fairy to the innocence of children playing. The phoenix flees the sprite for the company of the children and–

> "The Fairy to my bosom flew
> weeping tears of morning dew
> I said thou foolish whimpring thing

Is not that thy Fairy Ring
Where those children sport and play
In fairy fancies light and gay?
Seem the child and be a child
And the Phoenix is beguild
But if thou seem a fairy thing
Then it flies on glancing Wing."

See too the poem *William Bond* – fairies seem to represent natural, uninhibited love and desire. In *Long John Brown and Little Mary Bell* Mary's personal fairy mocks the devil for declaring that 'Love is a sin.'

These quite individual conceptions of the nature of faery were elaborated by the poet from the pre-existing folk materials of longstanding. We have just seen mention of fairy rings and, in one very significant respect, Blake did not depart at all from conventional imaginings of fairies: his creatures are always very small. There are numerous examples of this:

- An early poem, found in the manuscript collection owned by Rossetti, describes how "A fairy leapt upon my knee." Blake condemns it as "Thou paltry, gilded, poisonous worm," emphasising its miniature dimensions.
- In the poem *The Marriage Ring* fairies are called 'Sparrows', indicating clearly how Blake envisaged them as small and delicate, bird-like beings.
- In another early poem, found only in manuscript, 'Little Mary Bell' keeps a fairy hidden in a nut.
- An illustration for the 1797 edition of Gray's *A Long Story* has fairies riding upon flies;
- In *Europe* Blake caught the fairy muse in his hat "as boys knock down a butterfly" and then took it home "in my warm bosom" where it perched on his table and dictated the verse. In his early poem, *The Fairy*, Blake likewise catches a elf in his hat after it leaps from some leaves in an effort to escape. He addresses it as his 'Butterfly.'

- Lastly, in his famous account of a fairy funeral, Blake described "creatures of the size and colour of green and grey grasshoppers, bearing a body laid out on a rose leaf."

Blake's vision was, of course, a highly personal one and we would seldom be well advised to treat his version of fairy-lore as an authoritative guide to what his contemporaries believed about the supernatural world. Nonetheless, it is a fascinating and coherent conception and a notable element within his overall philosophy.

CHAPTER THIRTY

Fairies of Albion

WILLIAM BLAKE AND FAIRY ORIGINS

In the previous chapter I discussed William Blake's conceptions of the nature of fairies. From his illustrated book *The Marriage of Heaven and Hell* the text to plate eleven reads as follows:

> "The ancient Poets animated all sensible objects
> with Gods or Geniuses, calling them by the names and
> adorning them with the properties of woods, rivers,
> mountains, lakes, cities, nations, and whatever their
> enlarged & numerous senses could perceive."

I think it would be perfectly reasonable to regard this as an allusion to Blake's treatment of fairies as animating spirits of nature. He, of course, went far beyond this, elaborating this thought considerably in the *Four Zoas,* but in its original conception it coincided exactly with one of the commonest theories on the source of fairy beliefs. As seen in the last chapter, Blake's view of natural forces (and therefore of fairies) was that they could be harmful as well as productive; they are inexorable powers in unending strife. For this reason, fairies must be approached with respect and care; they must be propitiated and never taken for granted. They can be threatening as well as friendly, an understanding that Blake depicted well in his verse.

There are two books which particularly discuss the development of popular ideas on fairies. The first is the classic *British Fairy Origins* by Lewis Spence, published in 1946. Spence, who had a lifelong interest in the occult and mythology, set out a number of sources which he felt jointly fed into the fairy belief. These are that fairies were:

- *elementary spirits* – they are the spirits of natural features;
- *spirits of the dead* – fairies are, in a sense, simply ghosts. They haunt burial tumuli, the deceased are often found amongst their number (explicitly in *The Fairy Dwelling on Selena Moor)* and time spent with them can age the visitor;
- *ancestral spirits* – more than just being the dead, fairies were the dead of a particular family – the protective spirits of their predecessors;
- *aboriginal races* – this theory postulates that fairies are a recollection of former inhabitants of Britain who were pushed to the margins by later settlers. It is a garbled derivative of Darwin's ideas of evolution as set out in *The Descent of Man:* the elusive pygmy races are our ape-like ancestors. Of course, there is no evidence at all that Britain and Ireland were ever settled by any other than races of full stature and this is by far the least convincing of these origin theories;
- *former pagan gods* – it seems widely accepted, for example, that the fairies of Ireland are the much – diminished survivors of the ancient *Tuatha de Danaan.* Blake endorsed this theory.
- *totemic* – the fairies are symbols of tribal kinship with certain animals; or,
- *fallen angels* – they were cast out of heaven with Lucifer, but did not plummet all the way into hell (a widespread belief in Scotland on the evidence of Evans Wentz).

More recently, Katherine Briggs laid out the competing (or intermingled) theories in her book *Fairies in Tradition and Literature.* Her list is very similar to Spence's – fairies derive from:

- *forgotten gods and nature spirits* – they are the seasons personified and the spirits of trees and water. Amongst these Briggs includes fairies which may have been intended to act as warnings to children to avoid harmful places such as rivers, standing water and orchards – for example, Jenny Greenteeth, the spirit who lurked beneath the grass-like scum on pools, waiting to drag down unwary infants;

- *the 'hosts of the dead' –* such as the 'Wild Hunt';
- *fallen devils*
- *giants and monsters*, and,
- *tutelary spirits* which comprise ancestral spirits attached to a particular family (most notably the *banshees* of Scotland who warn of family tragedy) and brownies and the like which serve a particular farm or household.

In each list I have given priority to fairies as nature spirits. This animistic idea is part of what Blake seems to have been referring to in the verse quoted. The classical nymphs of wood and well, the *dryads* and *naiads*, are plainly the 'geniuses of woods, rivers and lakes' mentioned by Blake and very evidently contributed something to his thought and to our more general understanding of faery.

For British writers, at least, the different spirits were interchangeable. For example, the Scots poet Gavin Douglas, in his translation of Virgil's *Aeneid*, makes a direct substitution of one for the other. In tackling Virgil's lines "Haec nemora indigenae fauni nymphaique tenebant…" he gives us the following (my highlighting):

> "Thir woddis and schawis all, quod he,
> Sum tyme inhabyt war and occupyit
> *With nymphis and faunis apoun every side,*
> *Qwhilk Farefolkis or than Elfis clepen we,*
> That war engendryt in this sam cuntrie…
> Furth of ald stokkis and hard runtis of treis…"[42]

Blake also preserved some notion of fairies as ancient gods, judging and punishing human conduct. They are the causes of illness and blights: for example, there is mention of their 'little arrows' in *The Marriage Ring*. In this allusion to a semi-divine role, it has to be admitted that it appears that unrequited love is the main woe that Blake imagines that the fairies inflict, in consequence of which it seems that these arrows are as much Cupid's as those of any vengeful being.

Nevertheless, these supernatural beings have developed their own

---

42   *Aeneid* book 8, chapter 6, line 4 et seq.

local and distinct features and characters, in British folklore as well as in Blake's poetry. As I described previously, in William Blake's personal mythology fairies were spiritual beings investing natural features, but they took on other functions and aspects. Likewise, the British fairy tradition (both oral and literary) was woven from many strands and imbued fairies with multiple powers and meanings.

CHAPTER THIRTY-ONE

A doubtful tale from faery land

JOHN KEATS AND FAERY

Many writers have explored Keats' poetry and his interest in faery. A very good example is Maureen Duffy, *The Erotic World of Faery*,[43] which examines in detail the intertwined themes of fairy women, death, love, sex and Keats' relationship with his mother. In this chapter I will simply highlight some of the main aspects of the poet's treatment of fairy lore.

There is little doubt that one use of faery made by Keats is as a shorthand for girls and sex. Keats is open in his liking for women ("Nymph of the downward smile")[44] and feminine attributes, such as "Faery lids".[45] He readily goes further too, expressing his desire for physical contact. He "fondled the maids with breasts of cream"[46] and on a visit to Dawlish meets a Devon maid he greets as a "tight little fairy, just fresh from the dairy."[47] He expressly tells country wench Betty that he would like to "rumple the daisies" with her.[48] It isn't just a matter of lust though; fairies are linked too with love. Keats fears he will "Never have relish in the faery power/ Of unrequiting love!"[49] He also knows that fairy kind can love truly, just as humans do. At least amongst their own, the fairies will: "dance and kiss and love as fairies do/ For fairies be, as humans, lovers true."[50]

---

43   1972, pp.260-287.
44   *To G A W* line 1.
45   *Lines* line 7.
46   *To Charles Cowden Clark* line 34.
47   *Where be ye going* line 3.
48   *Over the hill* line 19.
49   *When I have fears* line 11.
50   *When They were Come to Faery's Court & Song of the Four Fairies.*

If you want a field guide to the fairy realm, Keats indicates that faeries are elemental spirits of nature (much as William Blake did). In the *Song of the Four Fairies* the supernatural beings Salamander, Zephyr, Dusketha and Breama are personifications of fire, air, earth and water. They are "freckle-winged" or have feathered or bats' wings and they are creatures of the countryside – particularly groves [51] and glades;[52] they are most often found at evening – for example in *Ode to a Nightingale* he describes how "the Queen Moon is on her throne, Clustered around by all her starry Fays."[53] Lastly, 'faery' is used by Keats (like John Clare) in the sense of diminutive and delicate.[54]

So far, so conventional; these faeries are the tiny sprites of Mercutio in *Romeo & Juliet*: they may be mischievous, but they are not wicked. Keats, however, knows that there are other strands of fairy lore, those derived from Celtic myth and from the fairy women of Arthurian romance – characters like Morgan Le Fay and Nimue. He is aware that fairies can be perilous and vengeful. In *When they came to the Faery's Court* he alludes to the 'three great crimes in faery land', which are sleeping in their company and stealing or disrespecting their property. This sort of disrespect will be punished – a very regular feature of human/ fairy dealings. The faery folk can be antagonistic and possessive: at the very start of *Lamia* Keats recounts "Upon a time before the faery broods/ Drove nymph and satyr from the prosperous woods."[55] The fairy folk are jealous of what they control and will not share – and it seems that this applies to lovers too. Diane Purkiss in her book *Troublesome Things* highlights the deadly privilege of being chosen and loved by a faery maiden. This is a traditional theme epitomised by *La Belle Dame Sans Merci*. She is alluring, this Lady of the Meads, "Full beautiful, a faery's child" with her long hair, wild eyes and sweet moan, but association with her is dangerous and almost invariably fatal. Contact with the lady is literally enchanting:

---

51   *When They were Come to Faery's Court.*
52   *To Emma* line 7.
53   *Ode* line 37; see too *To Emma* line 7 & *Song of the Four Fairies.*
54   see for example *Faery Bird's Song & Faery Song.*
55   Part I, lines 1-2.

"And nothing else saw all day long.
For sidelong would she bend, and sing
A faery's song… and sure, in language strange she said,
I love thee true."

Very soon the hapless knight was "in thrall" to the fairy and was deathly pale.

No wonder then that, in *Ode to a Nightingale*, the poet describes being "In faery lands forlorn."[56] Many of his descriptions of the fays imply carefree joy, but John Keats was also alert to the darker side of relations with supernatural beings, that their interest and affection could constitute a curse as well as a blessing.

---

56   line 70.

CHAPTER THIRTY-TWO

This Enchanted Isle

ROMANTIC VISIONS OF FAIRYLAND

On a recent trip to Glastonbury, I visited *Gothic Image* bookshop in the High Street and picked up a reprinted edition of their publication, *This Enchanted Isle* by Peter Woodcock. Originally published in 2000, the book describes itself as a study of 'the neo-romantic vision from William Blake to the new visionaries.' Woodcock has widely written on art and literature and has an interest in the 'shamanic' tradition; in this book he traces the influence of William Blake and Samuel Palmer on later writers, artists and film-makers.

William Blake saw all of natural life as being animated by fairies and he perceived elves and fairies filling the fields and hedgerows around his cottage at Felpham. In this, his acolyte Samuel Palmer was very similar. He was brought up on stories of fairies, witches and ghosts and imagined supernatural life filling the lanes and woods of rural Dulwich near his home in Walworth on the very edge of London. Later he moved to Shoreham, the Kentish village which inspired his finest work. As Palmer's son, Albert Herbert, later recounted in his biography, *Samuel Palmer – Life and Letters* (1892), part of the attraction of the rural hamlet was that traditional folk beliefs were still held by the residents there (and the painter also preferred the older pastoral poets for the same reason – their close links to romantic rural life). Palmer readily imagined goblins (that is, *brownies*) drudging in the thatched barns of Shoreham for the reward of a bowl of cream and happily listened to tales of fairies tripping across the domestic hearths. There is more than a nod to Milton's *L'Allegro* here, inevitable perhaps given Palmer's great admiration for his verse.

The mystical landscape visions of Blake and Palmer were inherited by various twentieth century artists, foremost amongst whom was Paul Nash. His writings disclose similar responses to the English countryside; he had a strong sense of the unique character of places and the power of those with links to antiquity. Of Wittenham Clumps, which he painted repeatedly, he said:

> "I felt their importance long before I knew their history... [The landscape was] full of strange enchantment, on every hand it seemed a beautiful, legendary country, haunted by old gods long forgotten."

Later in his life, Nash encountered the stones of Avebury. Initially, he responded to the forms and colours of the stones, saying there was "no question of animism here." This changed, however, so that in his essay for *Country Life* written in May 1937, *The Life of the Inanimate Object,* he was able to write "it is not a question of a particular stone being the house of the spirit – the stone itself has its spirit, it is alive." The idea of animating inanimate objects was very old indeed, "a commonplace in fairy tale and and occurs quite naturally also in most mythologies." In English culture, he wrote, the romantic poet Wordsworth played a major role creating a mythology that gave 'systematic animation to the inanimate.'

Sketching at Silbury Hill, he recalled that "I felt that I had divined the secret of that paradoxical pyramid. Such things do happen in England, quite naturally, but they are not recognised for what they are – the true yield of the land, indeed, but also works of art; identical with the intimate spirit inhabiting these gentle fields, yet not the work of chance or the elements, but directed by an intelligent purpose ruled by an authentic vision." For Nash there was magic in ancient and significant places that was still real and tangible, even in the mid-twentieth century. His art tried to express and to contact those deep forces of the English landscape.

Woodcock also links the Welsh born writer Arthur Machen (1863-1947) with the neo-romantic movement. Machen is best known for his Gothic horror novels, but like the others discussed, he believed that the humdrum world conceals a more mysterious and strange reality. Fairylore was just one element of his wide reading that he combined into his vision. In his second volume of autobiography, *Things Near and Far,* published in

1923, he acknowledges the rational explanations of fairy belief (later set out in detail by Lewis Spence in *British Fairy Origins* of 1946):

"I am well aware, of course, of the various explanations of the fairy mythology; the fairies are the gods of the heathen come down into the world: Diana becomes Titania. Or the fairies are a fantasy on the small dark people who dwelt in the land before the coming of the Celts; or they are elementals – spirits of the four elements: there are all these accounts, and for all I know, may be true, each in its measure."

Machen dismissed the more intangible of these scientific interpretations, but he was strongly attracted by the idea of 'little people' who still survived in out of the way places. They could provide a convenient vehicle for his peculiar form of horror. In *The Novel of the Black Seal* one character expands upon this:

"I was especially drawn to consider the stories of the fairies, the good folk of the Celtic races. Just as our remote ancestors called the dreaded beings "fair" and "good" precisely because they dreaded them, so they had dressed them up in charming forms, knowing the truth to be the reverse. Literature too had gone early to work, and had lent a powerful hand in the transformation, so that the playful elves of Shakespeare are already far removed from the true original and the real horror is disguised in a form of prankish mischief."

Thus in his stories the language of 'The Little People' is mistaken for that of the *Tylwyth Teg* and the physical traces of their culture and activities are taken to be 'fairy.' See for example the short story *The Shining Pyramid*: a girl thought to have 'gone with the fairies' has in fact been abducted by prehistoric and primitive cave dwellers surviving in the Brecon Beacons.

Despite this rationalism, albeit infused with violence and mystery, in his work Machen was also interested in the mystic, pagan, occult and romantic aspects of faery. Elsewhere he wrote that "belief in fairies and belief in the Stock Exchange as bestowers of happiness were equally vain, but the latter was ugly as well as inept." His work is thoroughly imbued with an awareness of and awe for faery; fairies may be illusory, but the mere suggestion of them endows his work with tension and glamour. Machen repeatedly makes reference to fairy languages and to the dread power of our supernatural neighbours, for example in his best known novel, *The Hill of Dreams,* and in the story *The White People.* In *A Fragment of Life* a bird sings "of the blessed faery realm, beyond the woods of earth, where the wounds of men are healed."

In Machen's unsettling and brooding story, *The White People,* a girl recounts strange magical discoveries in her secret journal. She describes meeting mysterious supernatural beings, such as 'the white people' and 'the nymphs.' She is taught by her nurse "the old words of the fairy language, so that I might be sure I had not been carried away." The girl also learns how to summon the nymphs and discovers that:

"I might meet them in all kinds of places and how they would always help me, and I must always look for them and find them in all sorts of strange shapes and appearances. And without the nymphs I could never have found the secret and without them none of the other things could happen ... there were two kinds, the bright and the dark, and both were very lovely and very wonderful, and some people saw one kind and some only the other, but some saw them both. But usually the dark appeared first and the bright ones came afterwards, and there were extraordinary tales about them."

Eventually, the girl goes to a pool and summons the nymphs. Previously, dipping her feet in the cold waters of the pool had seemed as if the nymphs were kissing them, but the tone then shifts in a sinister and menacing way: "The dark nymph, Alanna, came and she turned the pool of water into a pool of fire..."

In Machen's masterpiece, *The Hill of Dreams,* the hero Lucian becomes lost in a strange landscape: "all afternoon his eyes had looked on glamour, he had strayed in fairyland ...like the hero of a fairy-book." Ultimately he wanders into "outland and occult territory." Ancient hill forts are described as 'fairy-hills' and 'fairy raths' whilst the capital is imagined as the site of "dolmen and menhir ... gigantic, terrible. All London was one grey temple of an awful rite, rung with a ring of wizard stones."

Lucian's preference is for alchemy, cabala and Dark Age history, for "a land laid waste, Britain deserted by the legions, the rare pavements riven by frost, Celtic magic still brooding on the wild hills and in the black depths of the forest…" He wonders whether "there were some drop of fairy blood in his body that made him foreign and strange to the world." Lucian is drawn to the 'fairy bulwarks' of a Roman camp (the 'hill of dreams') and becomes bewitched by a beautiful young woman called Annie who speaks "wonderful, unknown words", apparently an unintelligible, possibly fairy language. She dismisses it as "only nonsense that the nurses sing to the children" but it becomes apparent that there is more to it than that, that it is in fact some form of enchantment.

Throughout this and his other books, Machen's descriptions of the Gwent countryside are vivid, intense and charged with otherworldly meaning. Lucian follows an unknown lane "hoping he had found the way to fairyland." He scrambles up to the old Roman fort crowning a hill near his home and falls asleep on a hot summer's afternoon, hearing "the old wood-whisper or … the singing of the fauns." This results, it seems, in his possession by fauns, nymphs or witches. He realises that he was been watched by unknown figures and that "they" are a woman and "her awful companions, who had never grown old through all the ages." Hideous shapes in the wood "called and beckoned to him" and it is ultimately revealed that Annie is somehow Queen of the Sabbath and a moonlight enchantress. She is no longer "the symbol of all mystic womanhood" as "jets of flame issued from her breasts" and she drinks his soul in an infernal, orgiastic rite.

PART THREE

British Fairies:
Themes and Theories

The Fairies Break their Dances

"The fairies break their dances,
And leave the printed lawn,
And up from India glances,
The silver sail of dawn.
The candles burn their sockets,
The blinds let through the day,
The young man feels his pockets
And wonders what's to pay."

A. E. Housman, 1922

CHAPTER THIRTY-THREE

Fairies or devils – whatsoe'er you be

THE BELIEF IN WITCHES AND FAIRIES

Fairies and witches have long been seen as linked and comparable, as the title quotation from Dekker's *The Spanish Moor's Tragedie* illustrates.[1] In his book on witchcraft, Geoffrey Parrinder observed that "there is undoubtedly much similarity between the activities ascribed to fairies and to witches."[2] These included the ability to fly, their preference for night time, their thefts of children and the foison of food and their ability to kill remotely.

These links and crossovers are of longstanding. For example, Chaucer in *The Merchants Tale* mentions "Pluto, that is the king of faerie"[3] and in the *Man of Law's Tale* equates an elf with a sorceress or witch.[4] Dunbar in *The Golden Terge* also alludes to "Pluto, that elricke incubus/ In cloke of grene..." (readers will note that he has of course chosen to wear the definitive fairy colour). One of the charges of witchcraft made by the English against Jean d'Arc was that she had frequented the Fairy Tree at Dompre and had joined in the fairies' dances.

By the sixteenth century the two beliefs were very confused and intermixed. Old women were accused of being witches and of flying in the air or dancing with the fairies, even though, as Reginald Scot pointed out, their age and lameness could make them "unapt" for such activities.[5] Fairies attended the witches sabbats and left rings on the

---

1   Act III scene 2.
2   *Witchcraft*, Pelican, 1958, p.71.
3   i, 10101.
4   Lines 754-6.
5   *Discovery of Witchcraft* Book V c.IX and Book XII c.III.

grass whilst the witches would visit the fairy queen in her hill.[6] Hecate, the mother witch and the queen of fairy all became compounded in the popular mind, as with the *Gyre-Carlin* or *Nicnevin* of Lowland Scotland; she rode at night with her court of 'nymphs' and incubi.[7] According to Reginald Scot, witches obeyed the commands of the fairy queen, Diana or Herodias.[8] Oberon became the 'king of shadows' in *Midsummer Night's Dream* and in a popular ballad was far more directly endowed with Pluto's crown, becoming "in fairy land/ The King of ghosts and shadows there."[9] It was believed that the habit of taking of changelings was because the fairies had to pay a tithe of souls to Hell each year. In George Peele's *Battle of Alcazar* "You bastards of the Night and Erebus, Fiends, fairies, hags" are summoned,[10] and in Spenser's *Epithalamion* there is this prayer:

"Ne let the Pouke, nor other evil sprights,
Ne let mischievous witches with their charms,
Ne let hob Goblins, names whose sense we see not,
Fray us with things that be not" (lines 340-3).

Just as prayers might avert the evil powers of fairies, their aid might just as likely be invoked: "Pray, fairies, grant, elves, that in fire of envie burne."[11]

In summary, hell and fairyland became essentially identical and for Reginald Scot the terms fairy and witch were interchangeable. Likewise for John Lyly, writing *Endimion* in 1585: for him fairies were synonymous with 'hags' and 'fayre fiendes.'[12] Similarly in the anonymous *Philotus* of 1603 a character can dismiss another in these terms: "Gang hence to Hell, or to the Farie"[13] and for William Browne a cave could be "An uncouth place (Where Hags and Goblins might retire a space)."[14]

---

6   *Daemonologie* c.V.
7   Sir Walter Scott, *Minstrelsy,* 'On fairies' IV.
8   Book III c.XVI.
9   *The pranks of Puck.*
10   Act IV, scene 2.
11   *The Shepherd's Dream,* 1612.
12   Act IV, scene 3.
13   Lines 122-132.
14   *Britannia's Pastorals,* book 2, song 4.

To this baffling mix the Reformation added another layer of confusion and prejudice. Puritans had two objections to faery. Firstly, it had to be accommodated with scripture and, as the fairies weren't angels, they had to be devils. Secondly, fairies were one of the impositions of Rome. King James VI condemned the belief as "one of the sortes of illusiones ... of Papistrie."[15] In Richard Corbet's *Rewards and Fairies* we learn that–

"The fairies were of the old profession,
Their songs were Ave Maries,
Their dances were procession."

Dr Samuel Harsenet, Archbishop of York, in his 1603 *Declaration of Egregious Popish Impostures,* called Mercury 'Prince of the fairies' and asked "What a world of hel-worke, devil-worke and Elve-worke, had we walking amongst us heere in England" when the Popish mists had fogged our eyes? Later he declared "These are the times wherein we are sicke, and mad of Robin Goodfellow and the devil, to walke again amongst us..."[16]

A rational few, such as Reginald Scot, dismissed the belief in witches as delusion and knavery, just as much as the dwindling belief in fairies, and felt sure that in time to come both would be equally 'derided and contemned.'[17] Sadly, such rationality was slow to establish itself and in the short term the witch craze swept Britain between about 1550 and 1650. Diane Purkiss, in *The Witch in History* (1996), has observed how fairy beliefs were converted into witch beliefs and were reproduced in the accusations and confessions of witches. In fact, a range of materials were recycled by people – plays, ballads, news, gossip, chapbooks – to create their own stories and to reflect their own agendas, concerns and conflicts. For example, Joan Tyrrye applied the common 'fairy midwife' story to herself, saying that she was blinded by a fairy she met in Taunton market. Others spoke of witches appearing dressed in green, the fairy colour. The problem was that, in the prevailing intellectual climate, old wives' tales of fairyland were no longer credible and were instead interpreted as accounts of demons.

---

15   *Daemonologie,* c.V.
16   pp.134 & 166.
17   Book VII c.II.

Some 'cunning folk' (healers and herbalists) tried to argue that through the fairies they only practiced white magic and that the supernatural help they received was only to cure and to do good. For example, Bessie Dunlop of Ayrshire was accused in 1578 of sorcery and witchcraft. She admitted that the fairies had helped her heal sick people (and cattle) and to find lost things. Likewise, Alison Pearson of Byrehill faced similar charges in 1588: she pleaded that a green man had introduced her to the fairy court and that the fairies had taught her remedies. Joan Tyrrye of Somerset swore that the fairies gave her only good and godly powers and showed what herbs would rid folk of witchcraft. John Walsh of Dorset said that he too was taught by the fairies under the hills to recognise and treat those bewitched.

Such justifications were very frequently advanced; other examples are Agnes Hancock of Somerset in 1438, Christian Livingstone of Leith in 1557, Andro Man of Aberdeen in 1597, in 1616, Elspeth Rioch and Katharine Jonesdochter of Orkney and, lastly, Isobel Haldane of Perth in 1623. All claimed to have been taught by the fairies, in Man's case by the fairy queen herself. Such a defence seldom helped the accused, even when the supernatural powers acquired were used to alleviate the effects of witchcraft or fairy affliction. Sir Walter Scott observed sadly that "the Scottish law did not acquit those who accomplished even praiseworthy actions, such as remarkable cures, by mysterious remedies."[18] For the accusers there could never be any 'good spirits'; the only explanation was that the suspected witches had consorted with the devil and there could be but one conclusion: Rioch, Jonesdochter, Dunlop and Pearson, for instance, were all burned. In the climate of the time, any contact with fairies rendered the person automatically a witch. By way of example, communication with the fairy court was a primary charge made against Alison Pearson and against Jean Weir of Dalkeith in 1670.

It is to be noted that gifts of healing and prophecy are *not* traditionally associated with faery. There are a couple of Highland examples of endowment with musical abilities and there is the fictional account of True Thomas the Rhymer, who was given seer's powers by the fairy queen (despite, as Sir Walter Scott puts it, his objections to "this inconvenient

---

18   *Demonology* letter VI.

and involuntary adhesion to veracity, which would make him, as he thought, unfit for church or for market, for king's court or for lady's bower"). That these supernatural attributes are ascribed to fairies only in witch trials is a strong indicator that they were being turned to as a less serious justification for the accused's former activities.

Witches were believed to have familiars who guided and assisted them. Academic and writer Diane Purkiss has suggested that stories told of brownies and other household fairies were reformulated by those suspicious of witchcraft and were understood instead to be accounts of demonic familiars.[19] This is definitely explicit in a pamphlet from 1650, *The Strange Witch at Greenwich,* that described the mischievous tricks of a particular spirit, such as throwing utensils and clothing around, along with "other such reakes and mad merry pranks, as strange as ever Hobgoblins, pinching fairies and Robin Goodfellow acted in houses in old times among Dairy Wenches and Kitchen Maides."

The records show that these familiars often seemed to have 'traditional fairy' names such as Robin, Piggin, Hob and Puckle (compare, for instance, Drayton's 'Pigwiggen' in his poem *Nymphidia*). Admitting regular contacts with a fairy would be interpreted and condemned as possessing a familiar. For example, Joan Willimot of Rutland had a spirit called Pretty blown into her mouth in the shape of "a fairy which should do her good." It then emerged from her mouth and stood before her in the form of a woman. Pretty subsequently visited Joan weekly and identified to her those of her neighbours who were "stricken and forespoken" (i.e. bewitched). Joan nonetheless alleged that her cures were wrought by prayer and not through the intercession of the fairies. She seemed to underline this by stating that the Earl of Rutland's son was "stricken with a white spirit" – the colour being one of those very frequently linked to fairies (see earlier chapter 5).

Anne Jefferies of St Teath, Cornwall, claimed to have been carried off to fairyland by six tiny green men where she was given ointment to cure "all distempers, sicknesses and sores" (such as the falling sickness and broken bones) and was also granted the power to make herself invisible at will. When she was arrested, it was alleged that these fairies were in fact

---

19   see *The Witch in History* pp.135-138 and *Troublesome Things* pp.153-4.

her imps or familiars. She strenuously denied this, saying rather that they quoted scripture to her, which demonstrated what good and godly spirits they were.

In some cases, though, the supernatural contact does seem more obviously to be evidence of black magic. Katherine Munro, Lady Fowlis, "made use of the artillery of Elf-land to destroy her stepson and sister in law".[20] Elf-bolts (flint arrow heads) were fired at pictures of her two victims, with the clear intention of injuring them. Similarly, Isobel Goudie of Nairn visited the fairy queen's court and saw Satan and the elves making the arrow heads with which Goudie and other witches then slew various people. Other such instances from Scottish witch trials are Katherine Ross, 1590, Christiane Roiss, 1577 and Marion McAlester, 1590. We can see here how fairy beliefs had become interchangeable with witch beliefs, so that elf-shot had been converted into bewitching.

To conclude, it is convenient to quote Sir Walter Scott in his sixth letter on demonology:

"With the fairy popular creed fell, doubtless, many subordinate articles of credulity in England, but the belief in witches kept its ground. It was rooted in the minds of the common people, as well by the easy solution it afforded of much which they found otherwise hard to explain, as in reverence to the Holy Scriptures, in which the word *witch,* being used in several places, conveyed to those who did not trouble themselves about the nicety of the translation from the Eastern tongues, the inference that the same species of witches were meant as those against whom modern legislation had, in most European nations, directed the punishment of death. These two circumstances furnished the numerous believers in witchcraft with arguments in divinity and law which they conceived irrefragable. They might say to the theologist, Will you not believe in witches? the Scriptures aver their existence;—to the jurisconsult, Will you dispute the existence of a crime against which our own statute-book, and the code of almost all civilized countries, have attested, by laws upon which hundreds and thousands have been convicted, many or even most of whom have, by their judicial confessions, acknowledged their guilt and the justice of their punishment? It is a strange scepticism, they might add,

---

20   Walter Scott, *Letters on Demonology,* letter V.

which rejects the evidence of Scripture, of human legislature, and of the accused persons themselves."

This rational analysis did many poor creatures little good: the Bible commanded that "thou shalt not suffer a witch to live" and those clinging to older traditional beliefs and practices could find themselves trapped and accused. In the early modern period the frame of belief had shifted and no space remained for benign spirits. Thomas Heywood captured this in *Hierarchy of the Blessed Angels,* when he spoke of:

> "...wicked spirits, such as we call
> Hobgoblins, Fairies, Satyrs, and those all
> Sathan by strange illusions doth employ..."

Fortunately for the hapless victims of the witch hunts, humanism and scientific rationality eventually displaced Protestant scaremongering. Nonetheless, once established, the associations between fairy and sorcery were hard to sever: it is surely no coincidence that Shelley labelled his Queen Mab as "queen of spells" in his eponymous poem.

CHAPTER THIRTY-FOUR

Sex and the fairy

FAIRY REPRESENTATIONS IN ART

As I have suggested in previous chapters, sex and sexuality are strong elements in (adult) fairy-lore. Maureen Duffy, in her extensive and detailed study of fairies in literature, *The Erotic World of Faery*, describes how fairies are an embodiment of repressed desires. Folk culture favoured greater sexual freedom than the church could sanction, and fairy tales allowed writers to deal with taboo subjects and taboo desires in an indirect way. Duffy notes that malignant spirits are more common than benevolent ones and she links the latter to a cheerful and open sexuality.

Fairy folk appear to have some kind of role as facilitators or instigators of human sexual relations. In the discussion of Queen Mab in chapter 8, I have noted her apparent role in instructing innocent virgins. Ben Jonson hints that house elves have some sort of role in enabling wenches to spend time with their lovers: in his *Masque of Love Restored* one of Robin Goodfellow's roles is to sweep hearths, clean houses and generally do the chores for the maids "whilst they are at hot-cockles." I do not think this is merely a reference to them playing the children's game akin to Blind Man's Bluff!

Even more explicit is John Lyly in *The Maid's Metamorphosis*. His fairies may be diminutive, but they having a knowing suggestiveness. Frisco tells fairy Cricket that "I wish I were a chimney for your sake." Joculo discovers that the third fairy is named 'little, little Prick' and replies –

"O, you are a dangerous Fayrie, and fright all the little wenches in the country, out of their beds. I care not whose hand I were in, so I were out of yours."

'Little Prick' then recounts his pastimes:

"When I feel a girl asleep,
Underneath her frock I peep,
There to sport, and there I play.
Then I bite her like a flea,
And about I skip."

I assume that the expressed wish to 'purse' the first fairy, Penny, also has a subtext, if only in the sense of pursing lips/ kissing.[21]

It is certainly undeniable that there is often close sexual dependency between fairies and humans. Fairy women often seek out human partners and the literary and visual representations of fairies are frequently more or less sexualised. Here, I want particularly to examine fairies in art in a little more detail, making particular reference to the twentieth century artists Arthur Rackham and Brian Froud. In *Victorian Painting* Lionel Lambourne describes how "many paintings ... [were] saved from indecorum by the pretence that the women depicted were not scantily dressed real women but innocuous fairies, tastefully 'veiled' in the trappings of allegory or myth."[22] This allowed artists to show naked and attractive young women without (once again) violating social taboos. I want to discuss Rackham and Froud as successors of this approach.

Both artists depict goblins in very much the same way – as grotesque, mischievous beings, often with a lascivious aspect in Froud's work. They also both depict fairies as being quite distinct – as female and human like. Nevertheless, there are significant differences in their portrayals. Rackham's fairies are young women with long hair, coy, slim, alluring and semi-naked or in see-through clothing. An example of this preference of Rackham's is an illustration to the story of *Rip van Winkle,* titled '*These fairy mountains.*' It depicts a scene on a peak in the Catskills range. One

---

21   Lyly, Act II, scene 2.
22   Phaidon, 1999, p.194.

cannot help but notice that, whilst the 'goblin' figures are fully clothed, in a manner suitable to the altitude and climate, the fairies are posed partially and only very lightly dressed, giving the illustrator a good opportunity to show us some juvenile semi-nudity. This apparently provides confirmation of Lambourne's observation on some of the parameters within which Victorian artists worked.

The uneasy equilibrium between 'cute' and 'coquette' persisted well into the twentieth century. Australian artist Ida Rentoul Outhwaite is a good representative of this ambivalence, with her pictures of winged prepubescent females with stylish permanent waves and short, if demure, frocks. By contrast, whilst Brian Froud's fairies are often young (though by no means always), they seem much more self-possessed or even self-absorbed. They engage with the viewer, they have their own sense of humour and their sexuality is their own.

Of course, there is nearly a century separating the pictures by Rackham and Outhwaite and those of Brian Froud and his art is likely to be 'post-feminist.' I'd argue there is more, though. Before there was sci-fi, there was fairy art, and the aim of both is to depict unreal things – generally as if they were actually real – either because the artist or the viewer (or both) wish to imagine it so. Fantasy art can portray things that are impossible (such as Froud's half-frog fairies) or it can present idealised images – how we would wish 'faery' to be; and it is often overtly sexual or suggestive of sexuality. Fairy maids were in the past allowed to be sexy because they were outside the structures of family and society (for example, they could independently choose human partners). They were allowed to express what would otherwise not have been permitted to the artist or to a young woman at the time. Those constraints are much diminished now and I think that explains the difference in atmosphere between Rackham's work and Froud's. The art of both is attractive, but the messages are very different.

CHAPTER THIRTY-FIVE

Full beautiful, a faery's child

AGE AND CONSENT IN FAIRY-LAND

"Oh, the fairies!
Whoa, the fairies!
Nothing but splendour,
And feminine gender."

The conventional conception of fairies is that they are female and that they are young and attractive. These are powerful and abiding archetypes; they make for good story lines, but they may also be a source of confusion in our correct analysis of fairy-lore.

Since Victorian times the dominant trend in fairy lore has been to make the fairies more and more diminutive – especially in theatrical representations. We may blame J. M. Barrie and Tinkerbell for this, but the miniaturising theme was far wider than just one author and may be traced very much earlier – see the references to "dwarfish" Oberon and to a "pygmean" race in earlier works. Keightley remarked, tellingly, on the fact that 'urchin,' a term formerly applied to fairies, is now only used of children.[23]

There have always been small fairies, but in earlier times they were generally conceived as being adults of small stature rather than infants of normal height. It must be noted that the term 'elf' popularly denoted tininess from the late eighteenth century at least (for instance in Blake and Keats). That notwithstanding, until the early nineteenth century representations of fairies tended to treat them as adults. In the case of painter Henry Fuseli, indeed, his fairy maids are women of a notably self-aware and unsettling character.

---

23   Keightley pp.319-20.

However, it was during the Victorian period that the representation of fairies degenerated through childlike figures to cloying cuteness. An interesting confirmation of this comes from John Ruskin, in his lecture on *Fairy land – the Art of Mrs Allingham and Kate Greenaway*.[24] Ruskin asked Miss Greenaway to provide him with a picture to illustrate his Oxford lecture. She warned him that her fairies would be "very like children" and, indeed, this was exactly what she provided. He showed his audience "two girlies, dancing outside of a mushroom."

During this same period, too, Victorian culture separated out 'the child' as distinct from adults and elevated the status of innocence in childhood. Previously children were merely small people; they have since become a separate social and cultural category. James Kincaid has argued that the modern concepts of sexuality were created by the Victorians as entwined with their notions of the uncorrupted infant. The result, he suggested, was that childhood and innocence have become idealised, fetishised and eroticised in everyday culture.[25] He asserts that writers such as Lewis Carroll and J. M. Barrie absorbed this erotic idealising of children and "drove it into our cultural foundations."

If we accept Kincaid's thesis, I would suggest that there have been a number of consequences of these cultural trends for our perceptions of fairyland:

- we have tended to lose sight of the former nature of fairies. As they have increasingly become little girls, some of the more sinister aspects to their characters have been elided;
- despite what I have just said, a powerful tension has arisen between the 'child' fairy and the earlier imagery – for example the fairies of Shakespeare and, even more strongly, Keats. The result was the projection of adult emotions and motivations and (my key focus here) sexuality onto fairies who were now often conceived as infants; and,

---

24   Ruskin, *Art in England*, 1884, c.4.
25   *Erotic Innocence*, Duke University Press, 1998.

- the nineteenth century use of children as fairies in theatrical performances, gave public visibility to girls acting on stage and, perhaps, portraying inappropriate roles.

Let me address the last point in more detail. Advances in stagecraft enabled Victorian theatres to offer magical spectaculars, with fairies flying, disappearing and posing behind veils of magical mist. Actresses had a reputation for lax morals, already, and there was some public concern over the impact upon the young girls employed to portray fairies. Would the exposure "convert them into coquettes before they have even reached their teens?" asked the *Pall Mall Gazette* in 1885. Regardless of the impact upon the girls themselves, Eileen Barlee in *Pantomime Waifs* (1884) fretted that they were "Dressed in the airiest and, alas!, the scantiest of costumes … and many were in flesh-coloured tights." They were presented to audiences as nearly naked or apparently so. The verse at the start of this chapter reflects this sense of sexualisation; it is taken from a music hall song and was quoted by Lionel Lambourne in the catalogue to the Royal Academy's 1997 exhibition of *Victorian fairy painting*.

These stage performances may all have been perfectly innocent in themselves, but the reactions of the viewers are another matter. I am reminded of Graham Greene's scurrilous and scandalous review of Shirley Temple in the film *Wee Willie Winkie,* published in the magazine *Night and day* in October 1937. He commented provocatively that Temple was being presented as "a fancy little piece" and a "complete totsy." Her admirers, Greene alleged, were middle aged men and clergymen who would respond to her "dubious coquetry." Their respectable predecessors of a generation or two earlier, the Dean of Barchester and Mayor of Casterbridge, may well have felt the same about Fairy Phoebe and her hosts whom they saw on stage. What is involved, perhaps, is a 'sanctioned' opportunity for adult men to regard the young actresses.

This may all seem hyper-alert, but let me give a few examples. Firstly, an account of a supernatural encounter recorded by Sir Arthur Conan Doyle in *The Coming of the Fairies* (1922). He supports his case for the reality of the Cottingley fairies with other evidence of their existence. He relates how two respectable gentlemen visited a hill in Dorset:

"I was walking with my companion ... when to my astonishment I saw a number of what I thought to be very small children, about a score in number, and all dressed in little gaily-coloured short skirts, their legs being bare. Their hands were joined, and all held up, as they merrily danced round in a perfect circle. We stood watching them, when in an instant they all vanished from our sight. My companion told me they were fairies, and that they often came to that particular part to hold their revels. It may be our presence disturbed them."

In a more recent version of the same event, there are some telling differences. The walkers witnessed: "a group of about twenty young girls ... naked except for a little gaily coloured short skirt that lifted up from time to time on the gentle breeze." The changes may well be entirely unconscious, but it seems to me that the tone here has changed from being a mere account of a curious experience; indeed, the tenor of the second version is not unique. Geoffrey Hodson was a theosophist and fairy-hunter who discovered elves all over Europe. He wrote of his journeys in two books, *The Kingdom of Faerie* (1930) and *Fairies at Work and Play* (1927). I will quote from each respectively.

- *Cotswolds, 1925* – of *devas* he says that "The actual form and manner are those of a vivacious school girl."
- at Geneva he tells us that "A particular fairy I am observing is a fascinating and charming creature ... The face resembles that of a very pretty young country girl." Another *deva* had the form of a "a fresh young country girl."
- in Lancashire in 1921 he was surrounded by dancing fairies, the leader of whom has a "form ... perfectly modelled and rounded, like that of a young girl." We are assured that "There are no angles in the transcendently beautiful form."
- a *deva* met in a pine forest near Geneva in 1926 was "like a lovely young girl, in thin white drapery through which the form can be seen." Another such is "definitely female and always nude... Her form is always entrancingly beautiful."

These descriptions may seem more conscious of sexuality, but a note of caution on this is provided by Diana Purkiss; she reminds us that:

"We in the post-modern world are apt to be convinced that sex is at the bottom of everything, that we know far more about sex than the Victorians did, and that we can read their unconsciousness like a book. These are all dangerous thoughts. Just because sex seems to us at the bottom of everything, does not mean that this is equally true for all others; just because we know a lot more about our own sexualities (and do we really?) does not mean we know a lot about Victorian sexualities; just because we read something in a text doesn't mean it is there for everyone."[26]

Despite these cautionary words, Purkiss concedes that some artists of the period trod an uncertain line between eroticism and harmlessness. She proposes, for example, that some of Cicely Mary Barker's *Flower Fairies* hover in this uncertain interstice. Mostly, these are demure illustrations, although sometimes perhaps Barker does allow what may be interpreted as some risqué off-the-shoulder looks. As I suggested in the previous chapter, Arthur Rackham too appears to have taken advantage of the 'value-free' environment of Faerie to indulge in pictures of girls in see-through frocks and careless deshabille; witness some of his illustrations of *Midsummer Night's Dream*. As discussed in that chapter, depicting fairies seems to have been treated by many artists as a licence to adapt classical nudes to a more domestic scene, a wisp or two of gauze maintaining an illusion of modesty and decorum.

Furthermore, it may be worth remarking that all these child like 'forms' (whether presented as 'art', on stage or in their natural surroundings in the Cotswolds) are simultaneously naked or scantily attired *and* independent of adult society. Those factors combined may well have served to liberate the response of some observers from the normal social and moral restraints. Without doubt, the consequence has been that we have ended up confused and uncomfortable with aspects of our fairy lore.

That said, the nineteenth and early twentieth centuries weren't all irredeemable tweeness amongst fairies. For example, Christina Rossetti wrote the strange and disturbing *Goblin Market*, a poem that, as Diane Purkiss neatly expresses it, "restores fully a sense of the otherness and

---

26 *Troublesome Things*, c.7 'Victorian Fairies' & p.261.

menace of the fairy world." More recently, the huge international popularity of Tolkien's stories of elves and dwarves has helped to provide a much needed corrective to the saccharine flower fairies of the Edwardian nursery. Legolas and Arwen have revived the Norse and Celtic traditions of human sized and mature fairies. Their robust combativeness and sexuality are a welcome reminder of older visions of the supernatural and are redressing the balance of imagery in the popular imagination.

Nonetheless, we are left with a puzzling dichotomy in the conventions as to representations of faery in the twenty-first century. A short search on the internet readily confirms this. On the one hand we have the sexy faery babe, as represented perhaps by in some of the pictures created by Bente Schlick. In contrast, there are the images of fairies as the embodiment of childhood innocence, for which I might suggest an image like 'Caught by a Sunbeam' by artist Josephine Wall. Lastly, there are the mature, self-possessed and possibly dangerous fairy women found in Brian Froud's work.

Fairy maids in corsets with heaving cleavages are not rare, but they are hugely outnumbered by the more fey images, it has to be admitted. The newly established convention, that fairies are perfect manifestations of physical attractiveness and/ or innocence, stands in stark contrast to older conceptions. Fairies maidens were renowned in folk-lore for their alluring beauty, but they often suffered defects that betrayed their real nature: they might have cow's tails, cloven feet beneath their long dresses, fingerless hands or hollow backs. These aspects of fairy nature are very seldom found now in the idealised portrayals that are so prevalent – Froud's pictures being something of an exception in their honest naturalism and occasional disturbing honesty about the 'average' physique (pot bellies and drooping breasts). The main problem with the paragons of prettiness is that they are one dimensional. Deprived of the darker and more dangerous aspects of traditional fairy nature, they become merely decorative – charming but devoid of deeper meaning.

In conclusion, it may be argued that our 'use' of the fairy myth has changed in recent centuries. Whereas fairies were originally the causes of unexplained events and a source of supernatural protection and help, they have increasingly become the vehicles for our fantasies – a convenient way of expressing issues that might not otherwise be tackled.

Recommended Reading

Anon.	*Round about Our Coal Fire*, 1734;
Aubrey, John	*Remains of Gentilisme and Judaism*, 1687-9;
Bottrell, W.	*Traditions & Hearthside Stories of Cornwall*, 2nd series, 1893;
Bourne, H.	*Antiquitates Vulgares*, 1725;
Brand, J.	*Popular Antiquities*, 1900;
Briggs, Katherine,	*Anatomy of Puck*, 1959;
	Dictionary of Fairies, 1977;
	The Fairies in Tradition and Literature, 1977;
	Vanishing People, 1978;
Burton, R.	*The Anatomy of Melancholy*, 1621;
Campbell, J. F.	*Popular Tales of the West Highlands*, vol.2, 1890;
Campbell, J. G.	*Superstitions of the Highlands and Islands of Scotland*, 1900;
Chambers, E. K.	*Midsummer Night's Dream*, 1896, Appendix A;
Cromek, R.	*Remains of Nithsdale and Galloway song*, 1809;
Delattre, Floris,	*English Fairy Poetry*, 1912;
Duffy, M.	*The Erotic World of Faery*, 1989;
Evans-Wentz, W.	*The Fairy Faith in Celtic countries*, 1981;
Halliwell-Phillipps, J	*Illustrations of the Fairy Mythology*, 1845;
Harsenet, Dr. S.	*Declaration of Popish Impostures*, 1603;
Heywood, T.	*Hierarchie of the Blessed Angels*, 1635;
Hunt, Robert,	*Popular Romances of the West of England*, vol.1, 3rd edn., 1903;
Keightley, T.	*Fairy Mythology*, 1850;
Purkiss, D.,	*The Witch in History*, 1996;
	Troublesome Things – a history of fairies & fairy stories, 2000;
Rhys, J.	*Celtic Folklore*, 1901;
Ritson, J.	*A Dissertation on Fairies*, 1831;
Rosen, B.	*Witchcraft in England 1558-1618*, 1969;

Scot, Reginald,	*The Discoverie of Witchcraft*, 1584;
Scott, Sir Walter,	*Minstrelsy of the Scottish borders*, vol.2, 1812;
	Letters on Demonology and Witchcraft, 1836;
Sikes, Wirt	*British Goblins*, 1880;
Spence, L.	*British Fairy Origins*, 1946;
Stuart, James,	*Daemonologie*, 1597.

Selected Verse

Young Tamlane

O I forbid ye, maidens a',
That wear gowd on your hair,
To come or gae by Carterhaugh;
For young Tamlane is there.
There's nane, that gaes by Carterhaugh,
But maun leave him a wad;
Either goud rings or green mantles,
Or else their maidenheid.
Now, gowd rings ye may buy, maidens,
Green mantles ye may spin;
But, gin ye lose your maidenheid,
Ye'll ne'er get that agen.
But up then spak her, fair Janet,
The fairest o' a' her kin;
"I'll cum and gang to Carterhaugh,
"And ask nae leave o' him."
Janet has kilted her green kirtle,
A little abune her knee;
And she has braided her yellow hair,
A little abune her bree.
And when she cam to Carterhaugh,
She gaed beside the well;
And there she fand his steed standing,
But away was himsell.
She hadna pu'd a red red rose,
A rose but barely three;
Till up and starts a wee wee man,
At Lady Janet's knee.
Says—"Why pu' ye the rose, Janet?

"What gars ye break the tree?
"Or why come ye to Carterhaugh,
"Withoutten leave o' me?"
Says—"Carterhaugh it is mine ain;
"My daddie gave it me;
"I'll come and gang to Carterhaugh,
"And ask nae leave o' thee."
He's ta'en her by the milk-white hand,
Amang the leaves sae green;
And what they did I cannot tell—
The green leaves were between.
He's ta'en her by the milk-white hand,
Amang the roses red;
And what they did I cannot say—
She ne'er returned a maid.
When she cam to her father's ha',
She looked pale and wan;
They thought she'd dried some sair sickness,
Or been wi' some leman.
She didna comb her yellow hair,
Nor make meikle o' her heid;
And ilka thing, that lady took,
Was like to be her deid.
Its four and twenty ladies fair
Were playing at the ba';
Janet, the wightest of them anes,
Was faintest o' them a'.
Four and twenty ladies fair
Were playing at the chess;
And out there came the fair Janet,
As green as any grass.
Out and spak an auld gray-headed knight,
Lay o'er the castle wa'—
"And ever alas! for thee, Janet,
"But we'll be blamed a'!"
"Now haud your tongue, ye auld gray knight!
"And an ill deid may ye die!
"Father my bairn on whom I will,
"I'll father nane on thee."
Out then spak her father dear,

And he spak meik and mild—
"And ever alas! my sweet Janet,
"I fear ye gae with child."
"And, if I be with child, father,
"Mysell maun bear the blame;
"There's ne'er a knight about your ha'
"Shall hae the bairnie's name.
"And if I be with child, father,
"'Twill prove a wondrous birth;
"For well I swear I'm not wi' bairn
"To any man on earth.
"If my love were an earthly knight,
"As he's an elfin grey,
"I wadna gie my ain true love
"For nae lord that ye hae."
She princked hersell and prinn'd hersell,
By the ae light of the moon,
And she's away to Carterhaugh,
To speak wi' young Tamlane.
And when she cam to Carterhaugh,
She gaed beside the well;
And there she saw the steed standing,
But away was himsell.
She hadna pu'd a double rose,
A rose but only twae,
When up and started young Tamlane,
Says—"Lady, thou pu's nae mae!
"Why pu' ye the rose, Janet,
"Within this garden grene,
"And a' to kill the bonny babe,
"That we got us between?"
"The truth ye'll tell to me, Tamlane;
"A word ye mauna lie;
"Gin ye're ye was in haly chapel,
"Or sained in Christentie."
"The truth I'll tell to thee, Janet,
"A word I winna lie;
"A knight me got, and a lady me bore,
"As well as they did thee.
"Randolph, Earl Murray, was my sire,

"Dunbar, Earl March, is thine;
"We loved when we were children small,
"Which yet you well may mind.
"When I was a boy just turned of nine,
"My uncle sent for me,
"To hunt, and hawk, and ride with him,
"And keep him cumpanie.
"There came a wind out of the north,
"A sharp wind and a snell;
"And a dead sleep came over me,
"And frae my horse I fell.
"The Queen of Fairies keppit me,
"In yon green hill to dwell;
"And I'm a Fairy, lyth and limb;
"Fair ladye, view me well.
"But we, that live in Fairy-land,
"No sickness know, nor pain;
"I quit my body when I will,
"And take to it again.
"I quit my body when I please,
"Or unto it repair;
"We can inhabit, at our ease,
"In either earth or air.
"Our shapes and size we can convert,
"To either large or small;
"An old nut-shell's the same to us,
"As is the lofty hall.
"We sleep in rose-buds, soft and sweet,
"We revel in the stream;
"We wanton lightly on the wind,
"Or glide on a sunbeam.
"And all our wants are well supplied,
"From every rich man's store,
"Who thankless sins the gifts he gets,
"And vainly grasps for more.
"Then would I never tire, Janet,
"In elfish land to dwell;
"But aye at every seven years,
"They pay the teind to hell;
"And I am sae fat, and fair of flesh,

"I fear 'twill be mysell.
"This night is Hallowe'en, Janet,
"The morn is Hallowday;
"And, gin ye dare your true love win,
"Ye hae na time to stay.
"The night it is good Hallowe'en,
"When fairy folk will ride;
"And they, that wad their true love win,
"At Miles Cross they maun bide."
"But how shall I thee ken, Tamlane?
"Or how shall I thee knaw,
"Amang so many unearthly knights,
"The like I never saw.?"
"The first company, that passes by,
"Say na, and let them gae;
"The next company, that passes by,
"Say na, and do right sae;
"The third company, that passes by,
"Than I'll be ane o' thae.
"First let pass the black, Janet,
"And syne let pass the brown;
"But grip ye to the milk-white steed,
"And pu' the rider down.
"For I ride on the milk-white steed,
"And ay nearest the town;
"Because I was a christened knight,
"They gave me that renown.
"My right hand will be gloved, Janet,
"My left hand will be bare;
"And these the tokens I gie thee,
"Nae doubt I will be there.
"They'll turn me in your arms, Janet,
"An adder and a snake;
"But had me fast, let me not pass,
"Gin ye wad be my maik.
"They'll turn me in your arms, Janet,
"An adder and an ask;
"They'll turn me in your arms, Janet,
"A bale that burns fast.
"They'll turn me in your arms, Janet,

"A red-hot gad o' aim;
"But had me fast, let me not pass,
"For I'll do you no harm.
"First, dip me in a stand o' milk,
"And then in a stand o' water;
"But had me fast, let me not pass—
"I'll be your bairn's father.
"And, next, they'll shape me in your arms,
"A toad, but and an eel;
"But had me fast, nor let me gang,
"As you do love me weel.
"They'll shape me in your arms, Janet,
"A dove, but and a swan;
"And, last, they'll shape me in your arms,
"A mother-naked man:
"Cast your green mantle over me—
"I'll be mysell again."
Gloomy, gloomy, was the night,
And eiry was the way,
As fair Janet, in her green mantle,
To Miles Cross she did gae.
The heavens were black, the night was dark,
And dreary was the place;
But Janet stood, with eager wish,
Her lover to embrace.
Betwixt the hours of twelve and one,
A north wind tore the bent;
And straight she heard strange elritch sounds
Upon that wind which went.
About the dead hour o' the night,
She heard the bridles ring;
And Janet was as glad o' that,
As any earthly thing!
Their oaten pipes blew wondrous shrill,
The hemlock small blew clear;
And louder notes from hemlock large,
And bog-reed struck the ear;
But solemn sounds, or sober thoughts,
The Fairies cannot bear.
They sing, inspired with love and joy,

Like sky-larks in the air;
Of solid sense, or thought that's grave,
You'll find no traces there.
Fair Janet stood, with mind unmoved,
The dreary heath upon;
And louder, louder, wax'd the sound,
As they came riding on.
Will o' Wisp before them went,
Sent forth a twinkling light;
And soon she saw the Fairy bands
All riding in her sight.
And first gaed by the black black steed,
And then gaed by the brown;
But fast she gript the milk-white steed,
And pu'd the rider down.
She pu'd him frae the milk-white steed,
And loot the bridle fa';
And up there raise an erlish cry—
"He's won amang us a'!"
They shaped him in fair Janet's arms,
An esk, but and an adder;
She held him fast in every shape—
To be her bairn's father.
They shaped him in her arms at last,
A mother-naked man;
She wrapt him in her green mantle,
And sae her true love wan.
Up then spake the Queen o' Fairies,
Out o' a bush o' broom—
"She that has borrowed young Tamlane,
Has gotten a stately groom."
Up then spake the Queen of Fairies,
Out o' a bush of rye—
"She's ta'en awa the bonniest knight
In a' my cumpanie.
"But had I kenn'd, Tamlane," she says,
"A lady wad borrowed thee—
"I wad ta'en out thy twa gray een,
"Put in twa een o' tree.
"Had I but kenn'd, Tamlane," she says,

"Before ye came frae hame—
"I wad tane out your heart o' flesh,
"Put in a heart o' stane.
"Had I but had the wit yestreen,
"That I hae coft the day—
"I'd paid my kane seven times to hell,
"Ere you'd been won away!

Traditional Scottish ballad

Farewell, Rewards and Fairies

Farewell, rewards and fairies,
Good housewives now may say,
For now foul sluts in dairies
Do fare as well as they.
And though they sweep their hearths no less
Than maids were wont to do,
Yet who of late for cleanness
Finds sixpence in her shoe?

Lament, lament, old Abbeys,
The Fairies' lost command!
They did but change Priests' babies,
But some have changed your land.
And all your children, sprung from thence,
Are now grown Puritans,
Who live as Changelings ever since
For love of your demains.

At morning and at evening both
You merry were and glad,
So little care of sleep or sloth
These pretty ladies had;
When Tom came home from labour,
Or Cis to milking rose,
Then merrily went their tabor,
And nimbly went their toes.

Witness those rings and roundelays
Of theirs, which yet remain,
Were footed in Queen Mary's days
On many a grassy plain;
But since of late, Elizabeth,
And later, James came in,
They never danced on any heath
As when the time hath been.
By which we note the Fairies
Were of the old Profession.
Their songs were 'Ave Mary's',
Their dances were Procession.
But now, alas, they all are dead;
Or gone beyond the seas;
Or farther for Religion fled;
Or else they take their ease.

A tell-tale in their company
They never could endure!
And whoso kept not secretly
Their mirth, was punished, sure;
It was a just and Christian deed
To pinch such black and blue.
Oh how the commonwealth doth want
Such Justices as you!

Richard Corbet (1582-1635)

The Fairies of Caldon Low

"And where have you been, my Mary,
And where have you been from me?"
"I've been to the top of the Caldon-Low,
The midsummer night to see!"
"And what did you see, my Mary,
All up on the Caldon-Low?"
"I saw the glad sunshine come down,
And I saw the merry winds blow."
"And what did you hear, my Mary,
All up on the Caldon-Hill?"
"I heard the drops of water made,
And the ears of the green corn fill."
"Oh! tell me all, my Mary,
All, all that ever you know,
For you must have seen the fairies,
Last night, on the Caldon-Low."
"Then take me on your knee, mother;
And listen, mother of mine.
A hundred fairies danced last night,
And the harpers they were nine.
"And their harp strings rung so merrily
To their dancing feet so small:
But oh, the words of their talking
Were merrier far than all."
"And what were the words, my Mary,
That then you heard them say?"
"I'll tell you all, my mother;
But let me have my way.
"Some of them played with the water
And rolled it down the hill;
'And this,' they said, 'shall speedily turn
The poor old miller's mill;
"'For there has been no water
Ever since the first of May;
And a busy man will the miller be
At dawning of the day.
"Oh, the miller, how he will laugh
When he sees the milldam rise!

198

The jolly old miller, how he will laugh
Till the tears fill both his eyes!"
"And some they seized the little winds
That sounded over the hill;
And each put a horn into his mouth,
And blew both loud and shrill.
"'And there,' they said, 'the merry winds go
Away from every horn;
And they shall clear the mildew dank
From the blind old widow's corn.
"'Oh, the poor, blind widow,
Though she has been blind so long,
She'll be blithe enough when the mildew's gone
And the corn stands tall and strong.'
"And some they brought the brown lintseed,
And flung it down from the Low;
'And this,' they said, 'by the sunrise,
In the weaver's croft shall grow.
"'Oh, the poor, lame weaver,
How he will laugh outright
When he sees his dwindling flax-field
All full of flowers by night!'
"And then outspoke a brownie,
With a long beard on his chin:
'I have spun up all the tow,' said he,
'And I want some more to spin.
"'I've spun a piece of hempen cloth,
And I want to spin another;
A little sheet for Mary's bed,
And an apron for her mother.'
"With that I could not help but laugh,
And I laughed out loud and free;
And then on the top of the Caldon-Low
There was no one left but me.
"And all on the top of the Caldon-Low
The mists were cold and gray,
And nothing I saw but the mossy stones,
That round about me lay.
"But coming down from the hilltop
I heard afar below

How busy the jolly miller was
And how merry the wheel did go.
"And I peeped into the widow's field,
And, sure enough, were seen
The yellow ears of mildewed corn
All standing stout and green.
"And down by the weaver's croft I stole,
To see if the fax were sprung;
And I met the weaver at his gate
With the good news on his tongue.
"Now this is all I hear, mother,
And all that I did see;
So prithee, make my bed, mother,
For I'm tired as I can be."

Mary Howitt (1799-1888)

Lightning Source UK Ltd.
Milton Keynes UK
UKHW022038030521
383060UK00011B/2207